## "You Sh_____ _____,
## I'll Show You Mine."

Sydney laid her cards on the table without even looking at them. Without any expression at all, Reese laid his hand down, too. She slowly lowered her gaze.

Three tens. And a one-eyed jack. Four of a kind.

She'd lost. Dear Lord. Two weeks. She had to work for Reese Sinclair for two entire weeks. Under his "personal supervision," as he'd put it.

Reese shook his head and chuckled. "You don't think I'm serious about this bet, do you? I was just having some fun."

She lifted her chin and narrowed a cold look at him. "I said I'd be here at eight, and I will."

A muscle jumped in Reese's jaw, and she watched as his eyes darkened. "Just remember, if it gets too rough for you, that I gave you an out."

"I can handle whatever you dish out," she said in a voice so serene it surprised even her. "What remains to be seen is if *you* can handle *me*."

Dear Reader,

Welcome to the world of Silhouette Desire, where you can indulge yourself every month with romances that can only be described as passionate, powerful and provocative!

Popular author Cait London offers you *Gabriel's Gift,* this April's MAN OF THE MONTH. We're sure you'll love this tale of lovers once separated who reunite eighteen years later and must overcome the past before they can begin their future together.

The riveting Desire miniseries TEXAS CATTLEMAN'S CLUB: LONE STAR JEWELS continues with *Her Ardent Sheikh* by Kristi Gold, in which a dashing sheikh must protect a free-spirited American woman from danger.

In *Wife with Amnesia* by Metsy Hingle, the estranged husband of an amnesiac woman seeks to win back her love…and to save her from a mysterious assailant. Watch for Metsy Hingle's debut MIRA title, *The Wager,* in August 2001. Barbara McCauley's hero "wins" a woman in a poker game in *Reese's Wild Wager,* another tantalizing addition to her SECRETS! miniseries. Enjoy a contemporary "beauty and the beast" story with Amy J. Fetzer's *Taming the Beast.* And Ryanne Corey brings you a runaway heiress who takes a walk on the wild side with the bodyguard who's fallen head over heels for her in *The Heiress & the Bodyguard.*

Be sure to treat yourself this month, and read all six of these exhilarating Desire novels!

Enjoy!

*Joan Marlow Golan*

Joan Marlow Golan
Senior Editor, Silhouette Desire

---

Please address questions and book requests to:
Silhouette Reader Service
U.S.: 3010 Walden Ave., P.O. Box 1325, Buffalo, NY 14269
Canadian: P.O. Box 609, Fort Erie, Ont. L2A 5X3

# Reese's Wild Wager
## BARBARA McCAULEY

Silhouette® Desire®

Published by Silhouette Books

America's Publisher of Contemporary Romance

**SILHOUETTE BOOKS**

<ta
</ta

ISBN 0-373-76360-3

REESE'S WILD WAGER

Copyright © 2001 by Barbara Joel

Visit Silhouette at www.eHarlequin.com

**Printed in U.S.A.**

---

## BARBARA McCAULEY

was born and raised in California and has spent a good portion of her life exploring the mountains, beaches and deserts so abundant there. The youngest of five children, she grew up in a small house, and her only chance for a moment alone was to sneak into the backyard with a book and quietly hide away.

With two children of her own now and a busy household, she still finds herself slipping away to enjoy a good novel. A daydreamer and incurable romantic, she says writing has fulfilled her most incredible dream of all—breathing life into the people in her mind and making them real. She has one loud and demanding Amazon parrot named Fred and a German shepherd named Max. When she can manage the time, she loves to sink her hands into freshly turned soil and make things grow.

To Cris Grace, the Queen of Cuisine—
this one's for you!

# One

Cigar smoke lay like a heavy hand in the small back office of Squire's Tavern and Inn. Four men, brothers, sat around the table, cards in hand, their dark gazes intent on the current deal. Gabe Sinclair, the eldest of the four, frowned at his luck while Callan, brother number two in order of birth, considered the possibility of drawing another king for a pair. Beside him, Lucian, brother number three, smiled inwardly at a pair of jacks and deuce wild, while Reese, the proprietor of the inn and the youngest Sinclair at thirty-two, all but did mental backflips over the three queens in his hand.

They were a handsome lot, the Sinclair men. Each of them, with their thick, dark hair and rugged good looks, had broken more than their share of hearts in Bloomfield County.

Some said that Reese held the record, though. He had eyes that made women forget to breathe. Deep green, like a forest, and curtained with heavy, dark lashes. And his smile. Lord, that smile of his could charm the stripes off a zebra.

It also didn't hurt that he was six foot three, solid muscle and had won the honorary award of "Best Butt in a Pair of Blue Jeans" three years running by the females in Bloomfield. Reese proudly displayed his silver-framed certificate on the wall right beside his plaque from the Bloomfield County Chamber of Commerce for "Top Restaurant of the Year."

How sweet life is, Reese thought as he clamped his cigar between his teeth. Three queens, a ten-dollar stogie and two fingers of Patron Gold tequila. He grabbed a handful of chips from his winnings stack and tossed them onto the table. He was on a date with Lady Luck and about to score.

"Five dollars says that pot is mine." Reese grinned at his brothers. "Again."

Lucian glanced up from his hand of cards and bit down on his own cigar. "You close that mouth of yours long enough and you won't have to put your foot in it. I'll see your five and double it."

"Too steep for me." Gabe threw his cards down and pushed away from the table. "Gotta go, kids. Kevin and I have a fishing date at the crack of dawn."

"I'm out, too. Abby's waiting up for me." Callan stood, and wiggled his brow. "Far be it from me to keep a lady waiting."

Reese stared at his brothers and shook his head. The Saturday night games were getting shorter and fewer since Callan had married Abby six months earlier and then Gabe got engaged to Melanie a few weeks ago. When they'd all been unattached, these games had lasted until three or four in the morning. Abby and Melanie were great, Reese thought, and he knew he couldn't ask for better sisters-in-law. He was happy for his brothers, but now the Sinclair reputation of devout bachelorhood lay in the hands of himself and Lucian.

And speaking for himself, Reese thought, it was a reputation he was proud to uphold.

"Looks like it's just you and me, Bro." Reese tipped his chair back on two legs while Gabe and Callan pulled on their jackets. "I see you..." he tossed a few more chips into the pile "...and I—"

The door to the office flew open.

"Reese Sinclair, this has got to stop immediately!"

Reese swiveled to look at the woman standing in the doorway.

Sydney Taylor.

Uh-oh.

Sydney's pale blond hair tumbled around her flushed face and fell in wild waves over the shoulders of the red-plaid cotton bathrobe she wore. She brought the crisp early November night air in with her, and the earthy scent of autumn leaves. In her arms she held Boomer, Reese's Border collie-terrier-Lab. Boomer was covered with mud. So was Sydney. All the way down to her fluffy brown slippers.

Mud on Sydney Taylor? Definitely a Kodak moment, Reese thought. He wanted to laugh, desperately, but the look of ice-cold fury on Sydney's face stopped him. She'd murder him if he so much as smiled. Everyone knew that Sydney Taylor could cut a man off at the knees with just a glance. She might be pretty, but she was so damn bossy everyone called her Sydney the Hun. Not to her face, of course. After all, she was the granddaughter of the Honorable Judge Randolph Howland, and that did deserve a certain amount of respect.

Reese glanced at his brothers. Based on their slack jaws, they were obviously just as shocked as he was to see the impeccable Sydney Taylor in her bathrobe, covered with mud, holding a dog in her arms. Somehow, even in her disheveled state, she had an air of royalty.

"Well, if it bothers you that much, Syd—" Reese brought his chair back down on four legs "—the game's just about over."

Narrowing eyes the color of blue ice at Reese, Sydney lifted one finely arched eyebrow and pressed her lips tightly together. "You know perfectly well what I'm talking about. Your dog was in my flower bed again."

Sydney had recently moved into the upstairs apartment of the historic brick building directly across the street from Squire's Tavern. She'd also rented the store downstairs and had been renovating to open a restaurant. She'd installed a deep-blue awning over beveled glass French doors and created a garden-like entrance. Hence the flowers which Boomer had become so attracted to.

"Are you sure it was my dog?" Reese asked innocently. "I could have sworn I saw Madge Evans's poodle out earlier."

"Madge is a responsible pet owner," Sydney said irritably. "You, on the other hand, are not. This is the fourth time in three weeks I've caught Boomer in my flowers. He's all but ruined my pansies, dug up my bulbs twice and chewed up my chrysanthemums."

Boomer barked, his guilt sealed when bright yellow petals fell from his jaw. Sydney stalked across the room and dumped the dog on top of the table. Boomer danced excitedly; chips and cards flew. Then Boomer gave a fierce shake of his long black-and-white coat and mud flew, as well. With an oath, Lucian jumped up, wiping at the splattered mud on the front of his white shirt.

Miss Lady Luck had suddenly been replaced by Miss Fortune, alias Sydney Taylor. Reese glanced forlornly at the queens in his hand, sighed, then threw his cards down and swiped at the dirt on his face. Boomer jumped off the table, sat at Reese's feet and looked up at his master expectantly. The dog's nose was covered with damp mud.

Reese knew he should be repentant, he really did. But there was just something about Sydney. Something about that haughty, patronizing air of hers that made him want to puff up his chest and bring that cute little chin of hers down a notch or two. Reese glanced at his brothers for a little moral support, but based on the gleam of amusement in their eyes, he was obviously on his own.

Reese stood and looked down at Sydney, considered telling her that she had a slash of dirt across her temple, then thought better of it. "I'll buy you some more flowers and bulbs."

Folding her arms tightly, she met his gaze. "What good will it do if your dog keeps digging them up? Need I remind you that my grand opening for Le Petit Bistro is in four weeks?"

Hardly. There was very little in Bloomfield County that everybody didn't know about everybody else, some of which was even true. Since Sydney had returned three months ago from culinary school in France, the whole town had been talking. Not about the restaurant she was planning to open as much as the reason why she'd left town over a year ago: Sydney had been left high and dry at the altar by Bobby Williams, Head Coach at Bloomfield High School. Bobby had been offered a position at NYU, only he'd neglected to mention the job to Sydney, along with the fact that he'd decided not to get married. At least, not to her. Bobby and Lorna Green, a cocktail waitress from Reese's tavern, had eloped on their way to New York.

No one had seen Bobby or Lorna since, but there had been talk that Lorna had been looking rather plump around the middle at the time she and Bobby had taken off together.

Reese had certainly never missed Bobby; he'd never liked the egotistical jerk, anyway. But Lorna, though a little dim-witted, had been a good employee, a rare commodity these days. Especially at the moment. With one waitress out on maternity leave, another on vacation, and a new girl who was sweet but couldn't remember what time to show up for work, the tavern had been in chaos for the past two weeks.

And now Hurricane Sydney had blown in.

*Nothing I can't handle,* Reese told himself and gave her his best smile. "I'm really sorry, Syd. It won't happen again."

"Spare me the charm." Sydney rolled her eyes. "I realize that works on most of the women in this town, but it's wasted on me."

From any other woman, Reese would have wholeheartedly risen to the challenge. But this was Sydney, for Heaven's sake. Sydney was starched stiff as a nun's habit. Going up against Sydney would be sort of like the *Titanic* taking on the iceberg. And those were icy waters he'd rather not swim in.

Except, at the moment, with her hair all rumpled, dressed in her robe and slippers, Sydney didn't look quite so starched or quite so stiff. She looked kind of…soft. Soft and cute.

Startled by his thoughts, he looked at her again, saw
the rigid lift of her shoulders and tight press of her lips.
Geez, what had he been thinking? Sydney Taylor might
be an attractive woman, but soft and cute? And those
frumpy robe and slippers she had on were not exactly
Victoria's Secret.

"Reese Sinclair, are you listening to me?" Sydney
narrowed her eyes. "I'm not leaving here until we settle
this once and for all."

"You could have him destroyed," Callan offered
from the sidelines.

Boomer jumped up and barked shrilly.

With a gasp, Sydney whirled. "I would never harm
an animal."

"Not the dog." Callan looked offended that Sydney
would think such a thing. "I meant Reese."

The look Sydney gave Callan could have wiped out
spring crops. Reese glared at his brothers. He knew they
were having a good laugh at his expense. He didn't even
blame them. If the situation were reversed, he'd want a
front row seat. With popcorn. But if he was going to
go one-on-one with Sydney Taylor, he sure as hell
didn't want an audience. "Weren't you all just leaving?"

"Not me." Lucian glanced at the cards still in his
hand.

"No hurry." Gabe started to take his coat back off
and Callan followed suit. "We could squeeze in a couple more rounds."

"Game's over." *And so's the show*. Reese snatched
the cards out of Lucian's hands, helped Gabe put his
coat back on, then shoved all three of his brothers out
the door and closed it behind them.

"Okay." Reese turned and faced Sydney. "Now, where were we?"

"You were about to tell me how you intend to keep your dog inside your own yard and out of my flowers."

"Oh. Right. Well, here's the thing." Reese glanced at the dog, then moved beside Sydney, lowering his voice as he bent his head close to hers. The scent of lavender mixed with something else he couldn't identify drifted from her skin. He hesitated, not only to appreciate the smell, but because he was surprised. He'd never thought about Sydney smelling so…nice.

Brow furrowed, she frowned at him. "What thing?"

"What? Oh, well, you see, Boomer's sensitive about being locked up. Ever since I found him out on the highway and brought him home with me, he gets depressed if I try to keep him in."

Boomer, who heard his name and seemed to understand he was the topic of conversation, lifted his head and thumped his tail on the floor.

"Depressed?" The tilt of Sydney's head signified her skepticism. "Maybe he requires more attention than you can give him."

"Shoot, Boomer gets more attention than a baby with a bonnet. He just can't stand to be fenced in. He needs to…stretch his legs a little."

"Gabe just bought the Witherspoon house," Sydney said matter-of-factly. "That's five acres of farmland, surrounded by several more acres. Plenty of room for a dog to 'stretch his legs.' I'm sure Boomer would be extremely happy there. He can dig to his heart's content."

"I couldn't do that to Boomer. He was already abandoned once when he was a pup. If I just gave him away like that, he wouldn't understand. He'd think I deserted him.''

She stiffened, then took a step back from him and lifted cool blue eyes to his. "Like Bobby deserted me? Left me standing in my wedding dress to face a crowded church on my own, is that what you're trying to say?''

Dammit, dammit. That wasn't what he'd meant at all. ''No, Syd, really, I—''

''Forget it, Sinclair. You think you can soften me up with that killer smile of yours and make me feel sorry for your dog, and I'll just go away. Well, I'm not going away.'' She folded her arms. ''Life is just one big lark to you, isn't it, including this bar you run.''

''Hey, now, this is a tavern, not a bar. There's a big—''

''Maybe you think I'm being petty, or that a few chewed up flowers are irrelevant, but your lack of respect for my property is irresponsible and insensitive.''

''Hey, I'm as sensitive as the next guy,'' Reese protested.

''If that next guy happens to be Bobby Williams,'' Sydney said, and pointed her chin at him.

That did it. Reese clenched his jaw. He wasn't anything like Bobby Williams. He'd had enough of Sydney's insults for one night. He glanced at Boomer. *This is the thanks I get for saving your sorry butt.* He looked at the table where cards and chips were scattered.

Irresponsible, was he? Life was one big lark, huh?

Well, fine, then.

''Tell you what, Syd,'' he said slowly, turning back to her. ''What say we let a friendly card game settle this for us?''

Her head came up, and her brow came down. "What?"

"A card game. Go Fish, Crazy Eights. Maybe a couple hands of Old Maid?"

His jab struck home. She straightened; her eyes shot blue daggers at him. "What on earth are you talking about?"

"A game of chance to settle this once and for all. If you win, I'll keep Boomer fenced in, and if I win…" *What did he need? Something to not only shut Sydney up, but put her in her place. Think, Sinclair, what do you need?*

He grinned suddenly. She'd never go for it. He knew she wouldn't. He just wanted to see the expression on her face, wanted to see her back down from a challenge.

"…if I win," he continued, "you have to come work at the tavern for a week. I'm short two servers right now. Wages included, of course, plus tips."

Sydney's jaw went slack; she was silent for all of fifteen seconds. "You expect us to settle this with a *card* game? That's preposterous!"

He grinned at her. "That's my middle name."

"You're serious. You're really serious."

"Yep." She'd back out now, Reese thought with smug satisfaction. No way she'd go through with anything as foolhardy as this. And since he had her attention, he'd up the ante till she squeaked. "Under my direct supervision, of course. You have to do what I say."

"What!"

"Don't go looking so hopeful, Sydney," Reese said, thoroughly enjoying the flush on her face. "I'm only referring to business here, though we could certainly discuss job perks and options, if you like."

"Let me get this straight." She blew a wisp of hair from her cheek. "If I win, you promise to take care of Boomer and keep him out of my flowers. If I lose, I have to work for you, here, for a week."

"Just three hours a day. Someone as tidy and organized as you could surely work three hours into your schedule."

Sydney's laugh was dry and short. "Even coming from Reese Sinclair, this is the most absurd proposal I've ever heard."

He knew she wouldn't go for it, but it had been fun, anyway. Still, he couldn't resist giving her pride one more tug. "If you're afraid to lose…"

"Afraid?" Her eyes narrowed sharply, and she stepped closer to him. "I'm not afraid."

"Okay." He shrugged and rolled his eyes. "Whatever you say, Syd."

"All right, Sinclair." That chin of hers went up again. "What do you say we make it more interesting? If I lose, Boomer's not only free as a bird, I'll come work for you for *two* weeks. If *I* win, though, Boomer not only gets kept in…" she leaned in close "…*you* have to come work for *me* for two weeks after my restaurant opens."

He gave a bark of laughter. "You're kidding, right?"

"Afraid *you'll* lose?" she asked sweetly.

"You mean it." He stared at her incredulously. "You'll actually go through with it?"

"I'll not only go through with it, I'll honor my bet, win or lose. Will *you*, Sinclair?"

A muscle jumped in Reese's jaw. "You're on."

"Fine."

"Fine."

They marched to the table and sat down opposite one

another. Reese scooped up the scattered cards and
started to shuffle them. It had been a long time since
he'd played Go Fish or Crazy Eights. He hoped like
hell he could remember.

"So what's it gonna be, Syd?"

She sat straight in her chair, her hands laced primly
on the table. "How 'bout five card stud, one-eyed jacks
wild?"

Reese nearly dropped the deck of cards in his hand.
"You want to play poker?"

"What did you think we'd play? Gin rummy?" She
lifted one brow. "My father taught me to count with a
deck of cards when I was two. When the other kids
were playing Chutes and Ladders, I learned how to double down with an eleven in blackjack." She smiled,
held her cool eyes steady with his. "Now deal the cards,
Sinclair. I'm about to kick your behind."

One hour and ten hands later, to Sydney's delight—
and Reese's annoyance—her stack of chips was twice
the size of his. It was a glorious sight, Sydney thought.
Each tall, neat column of red, white and blue signifying
her victory.

And Reese's defeat.

Of course, she hadn't officially won yet, but it was
just a matter of time—a short matter of time—based on
the past three hands. At the rate he was losing, she
should be able to put him out of his misery in the next
hand or two.

She still couldn't believe she'd let him goad her into
this. At twenty-six, she liked to pride herself on being
a mature woman, in control at all times, one who had
a solid handle on her emotions. A woman who used

logic and practicality to make decisions, not childish grammar-school antics of one-upmanship.

But he'd looked at her with such arrogance, such smug amusement, she'd simply accepted the challenge, as much to her surprise as his.

Glancing over the cards she held, she watched him study the hand she'd dealt him. Those incredible eyes of his were narrowed with concentration, and one shock of thick, dark hair tumbled over his furrowed forehead. Absently, he brushed his thumb back and forth over the strong line of his chiseled jaw; the quiet rasp of thumbnail against the shadow of his beard was the only sound in the office.

She'd never had the opportunity to stare so openly at a man before. It was not only rude, it was extremely forward. In this situation, though, she considered it a necessity. After all, this *was* poker. The most important rule of the game, her father had taught her when she was a child, was to closely assess an opponent. Every movement, every blink, every twitch, was to be noted, then analyzed. If her father had taught her nothing else before he'd left when she was twelve, she had learned to be observant. If she ever saw him again, she just might have to thank him for that one thing. But seeing her father again was one bet she'd never take. He'd called a few times, sent a couple of birthday cards, but he'd never come back once to see her after he'd walked out fourteen years ago.

Knowing what an extremely difficult woman her mother had been to live with, Sydney could understand the lack of visits. What she couldn't understand, what she couldn't forgive, was him leaving her alone with her mother, who had no one else to take out her bitterness on except her daughter.

But that was water under the bridge, Sydney thought with a sigh. She was twenty-six now and in a few short weeks she'd have the business she'd dreamed of for so many years. The past would be behind her, including the humiliation of Bobby and Lorna.

Sydney Taylor was going to be a new woman. She was going to be the woman everyone thought she was: confident, self-assured, poised. A woman who didn't give a damn what anyone thought or said about her.

All the things she wasn't, but desperately wanted to be.

Realizing that she'd lost focus of the game while her mind wandered, Sydney snapped her attention back to Reese. She'd learned that when he touched his finger to the cleft in his chin he had at least a pair, when he scratched his neck just under his left ear, he probably had three of a kind or better. When he brushed his jaw with his thumb, as he was doing now, odds were he was bluffing.

And so she watched him. Closely. Strictly for the game, of course.

She'd never noticed the scar just under that firm mouth of his, or the slight bump at the bridge of what she would consider an otherwise perfect nose. He wore his hair combed back, and the ends just brushed the collar of his blue flannel shirt. The sleeves were rolled to his elbows, his forearms muscled and sprinkled lightly with the same dark hair that peeked from the vee of his shirt.

No question about it, he was an amazing specimen of masculinity. He wasn't her type, of course. After Bobby, she'd sworn off smooth-talking, shallow play-boys who had more muscle than brain. While she could certainly appreciate Reese Sinclair's blatant maleness, she had no intention of being a victim of it, as were most of the women in town.

But then, Sydney knew she wasn't Reese's type, either. He went for the bubbleheads, the women who giggled at every joke and endlessly batted their eyelashes. She'd seen Heather Wilkins hanging on his arm last month at the pumpkin festival in town, then Laurie Bomgarden had been snuggling with him a week ago at the Women's Auxiliary's annual fall charity drive. Sydney doubted that Heather and Laurie's IQs combined was equal to the current outside temperature. And considering it was only the beginning of November, she was being generous.

But who Reese Sinclair spent his free time with was of no concern to her. Her only concern was beating the pants off that arrogant butt of his that the women of Bloomfield were so crazy about.

She glanced at the "Best Butt in a Pair of Blue Jeans" award he'd hung on the wall in his office. The conceit of the man, she thought with a sniff. Maybe they'd give *her* an award when she kicked that butt in poker.

"You vote for me, Syd?"

"What?" Realizing that she'd been caught staring at the award, Sydney snapped her gaze back to the table. Reese was watching her, and the amusement she saw in his eyes made her stiffen.

With a grin, he nodded toward the wall. "Did you vote for me?"

"Certainly not."

It was a bald-faced lie. She'd considered it her civic duty to vote when the ballot box went around for the annual "best butt" election. The contest had been close this year, between Lucian and Reese and the sheriff,

Matt Stoker. It had been a difficult choice, but in the end—she almost smiled at her own pun—she'd voted for Reese.

And she'd die before she told him that.

"Who'd you vote for, then?"

She straightened the cards in her hand, lining them up perfectly. "What makes you think I voted for anyone?"

"Sydney Taylor miss an opportunity to express her opinion on something?" He settled back in his chair and regarded her with a curious gaze. "So why didn't you vote for me? Don't you think I deserved it?"

She was becoming increasingly flustered by this rather personal topic of conversation. "I wouldn't know if you deserved it or not. I've never noticed."

"You've never noticed?" He looked slightly wounded. "You come over to the tavern every Wednesday night for the book review club. How could you not notice?"

"Reese Sinclair!" She slammed her cards down on the table. "In spite of your high opinion of yourself, I do not go to the book review meeting to stare at your butt!"

He looked at her for a long moment, then blinked. "Excuse me?"

"I said, I do not—"

"I heard what you said, I just don't under— Oh." He glanced at the wall, then back at her. "I was talking about the *restaurant* award. You are a member of the Chamber of Commerce, aren't you? And you did vote for the top restaurant in Bloomfield County, didn't you?"

The restaurant award. She felt her cheeks burn. He was talking about the *restaurant* award.

He clucked his tongue and shook his head. "Sydney Taylor, shame on you. Where *is* your mind tonight?"

Her entire face was on fire now, the heat spreading down her neck. "I...well...I—"

"I've never seen you stutter and blush, Syd." Reese gave her a lopsided grin. "You *were* thinking about my—"

"I was not!" She scooped up her cards again and stared at them. "The sun will be up in a few hours and you can crow all you want, Sinclair. Right now, this game is gathering moss. Could we get on with it, or do you need some ice for that swelling in your head?"

"You know, darlin'—" Reese picked up the cigar he'd put out an hour ago and bit on it "—that mouth of yours is going to get you into trouble one of these days. You need to learn to lighten up and have some fun."

"I am having fun." She smiled sweetly at him. "I have twice as many chips as you do. Bet's to you, *darlin'*."

Reese grabbed a large handful of chips and tossed them on the table, then grinned at her. "Five dollars."

It was a steep bet, the largest he'd made since they started playing. He was bluffing, she thought. She'd seen him brush his thumb over his jaw a few moments ago. Sydney matched the bet, then slid another column across the table. "And I raise you."

And then he scratched his neck under his left ear.

Oh, dear.

Now she wasn't sure.

She stared at her own cards. She had three jacks, ace high. A good hand, but not great.

His thumb brushed his jaw again. She chewed on her bottom lip.

"Let's have some real fun," Reese said casually and glanced up from his cards. "Let's bet it all."

*Bet it all?* Her throat went dry. "You're kidding."

"Nope." He shifted the cigar from one side of his mouth to the other and leveled his gaze at her. "Winner take all."

She knew enough not to look away, not to so much as glance at her cards. Confidence was everything in this game. Never sweat, never falter. Absolute self-assurance.

"Do you know how to make quiche, Sinclair? With a splash of goat cheese and a kiss of basil? It's a little more complicated than flipping burgers and pouring beer, but you'll get the hang of it." Without so much as a blink, she pushed her stack to the middle of the table. "Or maybe I'll have you put on a tux and wait on tables. There are plenty of people who'd pay to see that."

"Not as many who would pay to see you wearing a wench outfit toting a load of drinks." Reese shoved his chips across the table. "Hell, I'd give a month's salary for that, myself."

They stared at each other, neither one flinching.

"You show me yours, I'll show you mine." Reese raised one corner of his mouth.

Sydney laid her cards on the table without even looking at them. Reese glanced down. Without any expression at all, he laid his hand down, too.

Breath held, she slowly lowered her gaze.

Three tens.

And a one-eyed jack.

Four of a kind.

Her breath shuddered out of her. She felt a pounding in her head, as if her skull were a tin drum and someone was beating on it. Boomer, who'd started this whole business in the first place, lay under the table, softly snoring.

But she could hardly blame the dog for her own stupidity.

"We don't open until ten tomorrow," Reese said cheerfully. "But show up at eight to get ready for Sunday breakfast. The *Philadelphia Gazette* ran an article about the tavern winning the Chamber of Commerce award, so I'm expecting a crowd."

Numbly, she rose from the table, every limb stiff and cold. She'd lost. Dear Lord. Two weeks. She had to work for Reese Sinclair for two entire weeks. Under his "personal supervision" as he'd put it.

She couldn't think right now. Couldn't let Reese see how completely humiliated she was.

She'd never let anyone see her like that again.

"All right, then." Drawing in a deep breath, she tightened the belt of her robe. "Eight o'clock it is."

"Sydney." Reese shook his head and chuckled. "You don't think I was serious about this, do you? I was just having some fun."

She lifted her chin and narrowed a cold look at him, praying he wouldn't see how badly her hands were shaking. "That's just one difference between you and me, Reese. Everything's a big lark to you, a game. You don't take anything seriously, where as I intend to honor my bet and the deal we made. I said I'd be here at eight, and I will."

A muscle jumped in Reese's jaw, and she watched as his eyes darkened. "Have it your way, Syd," he said with a shrug. "Just remember if it gets too rough for you, that I gave you an out."

"I can handle whatever you dish out," she said in a

voice so serene it surprised even her. ''What remains to be seen is if you can handle me.''

His brow shot up at that, and she simply smiled, turned on her muddy, slippered feet and walked calmly out the door.

She intended to give Reese Sinclair two weeks in his life that he'd never forget.

# Two

___

Sunday was the only morning that Reese allowed himself to sleep in. He cherished that day, was grateful that he had a manager like Corky to come in early, start the coffee brewing, the grills heating, and the cinnamon rolls baking. Squire's Tavern and Inn was well-known not only for their hamburgers and pizza, but also for their breakfasts—plump sausages, country potatoes, biscuits that melted in your mouth and eggs so fresh they were still warm from the nest. He loved the smells and the sounds of his business: the food grilling, people laughing, having a good time while they ate and talked.

It reminded him of meals in his house when he was a kid. With five kids at the table—four of them boys—you had to yell to be heard over dinner in the Sinclair house. His father had always joined in with his children's antics, while his mother frowned and made a convincing effort to keep order. But as strict and rigid as she'd tried to be, they'd have her laughing and acting silly right along with the rest of them before the meal was over.

He missed those meals almost as much as he missed his parents. Twelve years had passed since the car accident that had taken them both. Sometimes it seemed like only yesterday, other times it seemed like an eternity.

Yawning, he rolled into the softness of the mattress and his pillow, cracked one eye open to glance at the bedside clock. Eight o'clock. He frowned and slammed his eye closed again, shutting out the early-morning light that poured through the open slats of his wooden blinds. He was up every other morning by six, but he never woke up before nine-thirty on Sunday. He still had an hour and a half to go, and he intended to savor every minute of it. The cottage he lived in was directly behind the tavern, a redbrick carriage house he'd converted into living quarters after he'd bought the abandoned tavern and completely renovated it four years ago. He was close enough to his business to handle whatever problems might arise, but it offered enough privacy for him to have alone time when he needed it. Or to entertain company.

Specifically, female company.

He was a man who fully appreciated women. The female gender, with their exotic smells and delicious curves, fascinated him almost as much as they intrigued him. They were complicated and mysterious; sweet and coy one minute, difficult and confusing the next. An absolute enigma that completely enchanted him.

Fortunately for him, women enjoyed his company as much as he enjoyed theirs. He understood the game well enough to know that, as an unattached male, he was open season for all the single women. But he was honest and up front with every woman he dated: he wasn't looking for marriage. Still, they had a way of pausing at jewelry-store windows, dragging him to movies that included at least one wedding, and somehow ending up in the department store housewares section, specifically china and silver.

But he was content with his life exactly as it was. He loved his business and his freedom. No one telling him what to do or when to do it. He never had to answer to anyone. No complications, no problems—

He buried his head in his pillow and groaned.

Except for Sydney Taylor.

Damn.

Sydney was one *big* problem.

He'd really never expected her to take him seriously when he'd made that bet with her, and he'd certainly never expected her to know how to play poker, let alone be so good at the game. But if there was one thing predictable about Sydney, it was the fact that she was unpredictable. He knew he never should have challenged her like that, but once he had, and she'd refused to back down, he couldn't just walk away. A guy had his pride, after all, and Sydney had tweaked his.

Knowing the woman, she was probably in the kitchen with Corky right now, telling him what to do and how to do it. Corky would have a fit about that, Reese knew. The man had been in the New York restaurant business for twenty-five years before he'd given up the fast pace of the big city and moved to Bloomfield. He'd applied for the position of chief cook and bottle washer one week before Squire's Tavern and Inn had opened its doors. For the past four years, Corky had been more like a partner to Reese than an employee, and even more, he'd been a good friend.

But Corky was particular about his kitchen. He had his own way of doing things. He wouldn't like Sydney messing with his pots and pans. Reese could see her now, with that stubborn little chin of hers pointed at Corky while she informed him of the proper method of cracking an egg or peeling a potato. That long, slender neck stretched high as she swished him out of her way. That sassy mouth giving orders.

Reese had known Sydney most of his life, but had never noticed before last night what a perfect mouth she had. Her lips were wide and full, rosy pink. She didn't know she did it, but every time she'd have a mediocre hand, she'd catch that lush bottom lip of hers between her perfectly straight, perfectly white teeth and nibble. More than once, that little action had distracted him. Then he'd remind himself he was thinking lustful thoughts about *Sydney,* of all people, and force his mind back to the game.

But he'd never seen her with that blond hair all mussed up like that, or streaks of mud on that smooth, porcelain skin. And he'd certainly never seen her in a bathrobe. As plain as the garment had been, there'd been something appealing about that red-plaid robe. Something strangely…sexy. Something that made him curious about what she wore *under* that robe.

And further still, what was under that.

Good Lord. He flipped onto his back and snorted. His brothers would have a good laugh if they could hear his thoughts about Sydney. Reese decided he needed to start dating more. He hadn't had much time for female companionship the past several weeks, and even Sydney was starting to look good to him. And that was ridiculous. Sydney Taylor was not even close to the type of woman he was interested in. Sydney was too uptight, too bossy, too—

"Are you going to sleep all day, Sinclair, or do you think we can get started?"

"*What the*—" On an oath, his eyes popped open. Arms folded, Sydney stood in his open bedroom door, a smile on those lips he'd been so foolishly fantasizing about and a gleam in her baby-blue eyes.

He was going to strangle her.

Eyes narrowed, he sat slowly. *This* was the Sydney he knew. Dressed in tailored black slacks, a pale blue, high-necked turtleneck that made her eyes shine, her hair pulled up tight in a smooth, golden knot on top of her head.

While, he, on the other hand, was buck naked under his sheets.

"Have you ever heard of knocking?"

"I did knock." Diamond studs sparkled on her earlobes as she tipped her head. "Twice, as a matter of fact. Corky told me to come on in if you didn't answer."

He decided he'd strangle Corky right after he finished with Sydney.

"This is my *bedroom.* You want to be specific about what it is you'd like to get *started?*"

"My duties, of course. What else would I possibly be talking about?"

He slipped down between the sheets and his white down comforter, plumped his pillow with his fist as he turned his back to her. "I sleep in on Sundays. Corky will show you what to do."

"Not a chance, Sinclair. Our bet was that I was to work under *your* supervision."

"Well, Syd, since I'm in my bed, what work under me would you suggest?"

"Why, Reese Sinclair." Sydney's voice dripped Southern debutante. "Sweet words like that do make a girl's heart flutter."

"If the girl had a heart," he muttered.

He heard her soft laughter and couldn't resist glancing over his shoulder to watch as she strolled around his bedroom, first inspecting a baseball trophy from the year his college team had won the state championship—he'd been pitcher—then squinting as she bent over his dresser and closely examined an oak-framed photograph of his sister Cara and her husband Ian that had been taken at their wedding last year, then another picture of his brother Callan and his wife Abby taken at their wedding six months ago.

She straightened, not even pretending to hide her curiosity as she continued to inspect his bedroom.

The woman was unbelievable.

"Tours don't begin until ten." Reese glared at her. "You can purchase tickets at the front desk."

Sydney smiled. "I'm sorry. It's just so overwhelming to be in the legendary Sinclair den of carnal delights. I expected to be stepping over the writhing bodies of scantily clad women."

"The maid cleaned up already this morning," he said dryly. "But there might still be a couple in the closet if you'd care to look."

She was actually heading for his closet when she stopped suddenly at the floor-to-ceiling bookcase he'd built beside an existing brick fireplace.

"Books!" she exclaimed. "You actually have *books* in here. Grisham, King, Follett—oh!" Her eyes lit up.

"Dickens and Shakespeare, too. Were they all left here by the previous owner?"

The sarcasm under that sweet smile of hers had Reese bristling. It wasn't bad enough she'd invaded his bedroom, now she was insulting his intellect. He'd read every one of those books, even had a signed copy of Fitzgerald's *The Great Gatsby* and Steinbeck's *Cannery Row*. His most recent purchase, though, and his most prized, was a first edition, leather-bound Alexandre Dumas *The Three Musketeers*. It had cost him a bundle, but it was worth every penny.

Still, he did have an image to maintain.

"Yeah, well, my comic books didn't take up much room and I needed something on the shelves." He sat, bent one knee while he stretched his arms wide. The comforter slipped down to his stomach. Sydney looked in his direction, and to his smug satisfaction, her eyes widened and she gasped.

Ha. That ought to send her running.

"Reese," she whispered, her voice filled with reverence. "How magnificent!"

Good Lord. Reese felt his face warm. He pulled the comforter back up as she hurried across the room toward him. Geez. He'd heard a lot of compliments, but never had a woman been quite so…exuberant.

"It's Louis XV, isn't it?" She stopped at the foot of his bed, touched one corner of his four-poster bed and ran her fingers over the dark grain. "Black walnut, right?"

"Ah, yeah." She was enthralled with his *bed,* for God's sake. He wasn't sure if he was relieved or annoyed. He watched as she stroked her fingertips over the round top of the smooth wood and made a small *O* with those pretty lips of hers.

His throat went dry.

"These rose carvings are amazing." Her fingers glided over the intricate petals and leaves. "Has it been refinished or is this the original stain?"

He dragged his gaze from those slender hands of hers and swallowed hard. What had she asked him? If the bed had been refinished? He had no idea. He'd just bought it last month at the Witherspoon estate auction after Cara had insisted it would be perfect for the inn. On a whim, he'd kept the bed for himself instead. Sydney was the first woman who had been in his bedroom since he'd set it up, but if it had this effect on all females, he would have to give his sister his undying gratitude.

Somehow, though, he couldn't imagine any of the women he'd invited here—and there weren't nearly as many as the gossipmongers proclaimed—noticing the grain of wood on his bed. He *did* know, however, that not one woman had ever commented on his book collection before.

He frowned as he remembered that Sydney's comment had been less than complimentary. And he certainly hadn't invited her here, either.

She bent on her knees and leaned closer still to inspect the carving, her hands moving over the post. Stroking. Up, down. Reese felt an arrow of liquid heat shoot straight to his groin.

Good God, as ridiculous as it was, the woman was turning him on!

"Gee, Syd—" Reese feigned a lightness to his voice, even though his entire body was wound up tighter than a steel spring "—now that you're such good friends, maybe you'd like me to leave so you can be alone here with Louis."

Sydney's head shot up as she obviously realized how...*intimate* her inspection of his bedpost had been. Her blue eyes widened for a fraction of a second, then she quickly dropped her hands and turned her lips up in what Reese could only call a smirk.

"Why, Reese Sinclair, you're upset because I got more excited over an old bed than you." She tilted her head to the side and touched her chin with her finger. "Don't take it personal, but you're just not my type, that's all."

Oh, was that right? Not her type, huh? She was just so damn pompous, Reese couldn't resist messing with her. Resting an arm on his bent knee, he lifted one dark brow and grinned at her. "You sure about that, Syd?" he said huskily. "If you'd let yourself loosen up just a little bit, I bet I could tip your tiara."

"Not a chance, Sinclair. But thanks for the offer, anyway. I'm sure you considered it quite generous on your part." With that, she turned on her heels and headed for the door. "By the way, I have some great ideas on improving the efficiency of your kitchen. Shouldn't take me more than a couple of days, then we can talk about developing a new menu. You really could use a little more variety."

She waltzed through the bedroom door in that regal manner of hers and Reese almost felt as if he'd been dismissed. The woman was enough to make a man chew nails and spit rust.

He frowned. What the hell did she mean, develop a new menu? He had a terrific menu, with plenty of variety, if he did say so himself. Why fix it if it ain't broke? And besides, she was supposed to be doing what *he* said, not messing with his menu or improving the efficiency of his kitchen.

Oh, no. The kitchen. If Sydney started rearranging things in the kitchen, Corky would kill him. He had to get down there before the woman caused too much trouble or any blood was shed, though that blood was probably going to be his own, Reese knew.

Whatever Corky did to him—and it was probably going to be painful—Reese figured he'd earned it. It was his own stupidity that had started this ridiculous bet. He'd made his own bed, so the saying went, and he'd have to sleep in it.

But the thought of beds brought his mind back around to the look in Sydney's eyes as she'd admired his. Those lips of hers that had gone soft, those long, slender fingers moving on the bedpost....

Dammit! He bet she'd done that on purpose, just to get to him. Well, he refused to let Sydney Taylor get the better of him. He wasn't interested in her like that, anymore than she was interested in him.

But now that he thought about it, when she'd told him that he wasn't her type, she'd tilted her head and touched her chin. Exactly what she'd done last night every time she'd bluffed.

Nah. Reese laughed at the possibility of anything more than an adversarial relationship with Sydney. Besides, as annoying as it was, it was also great fun sparring with her. Why spoil a good thing?

Boomer chose that moment to come bounding through the open bedroom door. With a shrill bark, he jumped on the bed and slipped his head under Reese's hand.

"Thanks a lot, pal." Reese rubbed the dog's ear. "This is all your fault I've got Sydney the Hun driving me insane."

Boomer slapped his tail on the blanket.

Shaking his head, Reese chuckled as he slipped out of bed. If there was one thing he could be certain of, the next two weeks were certainly going to be interesting.

War had been declared, and there was no question in Reese's mind who the victor would be.

Outside Reese's small carriage house, Sydney leaned back against the closed front door. Beside a black wrought-iron porch column, one large pot of rose-pink bouvardia sweetly scented the cool morning air, and a family of sparrows chattered excitedly in a nearby maple. Weathered clay pots of flowering cabbage dotted the moss-lined brick walkway that led back to the tavern, and a rusted metal tub nestled beside a concrete bench spilled the fading blooms of purple crocus.

Any other time, Sydney would have stopped to admire the beauty of the English-style garden with its double-tiered fountain and rose arbor. She'd had no idea such a lovely spot existed behind the tavern. But then, she'd never been in Reese Sinclair's bedroom before, either.

Her senses still reeled from the experience.

Closing her eyes, she drew in a slow, calming breath. Even now, outside in the fresh morning air, she could still see him as vividly as when she'd stood in his bedroom. The blush she'd managed to hold back inside now bloomed on her cheeks. Her skin felt warm and tingly. Heavens, but the man was something incredible to look at. Long and lean, with broad shoulders and a wide chest sprinkled with coarse, dark hair. His arms were muscled, his stomach tapered, without an ounce of fat.

When the blanket had slipped down, her heart had

skipped rope. He'd been naked under those covers, she was certain of that, and standing in his bedroom, surrounded by that masculine scent of him, staring into his sleepy, sexy eyes, she'd found it difficult to breathe.

And then she'd wondered what it would be like between those warm, rumpled sheets with him. What those sculpted muscles would feel like under her hands, how his tall, hard body would fit against her own.

She'd distracted those wayward thoughts by fawning over his bed. It was a beautiful piece of furniture, but the only reason she'd known specifics was because she'd actually been at the auction and she'd admired it then, as well. She'd picked up a French Victorian buffet herself that she intended to use in the entry of her restaurant.

But that buffet had definitely not been on her mind when she'd been kneeling beside Reese's bed. In spite of her yammering on about carvings and stains, she'd had more lascivious thoughts in mind. And she'd walk naked through a blizzard before she'd let Reese know that.

Honestly. If the man's empty head got any bigger, he'd have to wear lead shoes on a warm day to keep from floating away. The *last* thing Reese Sinclair needed was another female admirer. And the *last* thing she needed was to have her head turned by a superficial, immature rake whose single most recurring thought was about sex.

Tip her tiara, indeed.

Not likely.

Squaring her shoulders, she marched back to the tavern, determined not only to honor her end of this ridiculous bargain, but to put all prurient thoughts about Reese Sinclair out of her mind.

She hadn't spent nine months in culinary school and restaurant training for nothing. Squire's Tavern was distinctly eighteenth-century English: Tudor design with dark woods, rough-hewn oak beams, peg and groove floors, and a massive stone fireplace. There was a warmth to the tavern that welcomed its customers, and the food was very good. She was particular to the hamburgers and French fries herself.

Still, that didn't mean there weren't areas that could stand a little improvement. A tweak here, a nip there. Why not pass along a few of the ideas that had popped into her head as she'd walked through the main restaurant area this morning?

And anyway, Sydney thought as she let herself in the back door of the tavern, no matter what she did, Reese probably wouldn't notice at all.

# Three

_____

"**W**ho the *hell* put tablecloths on these tables?"

Fists on his hips, Reese stood in the center of the tavern and glanced around the room. Crisp, white linen tablecloths covered the black oak plank tables. In the center of every table, small crystal vases each held one single pink rose. Though he kept the tablecloths and vases in his back storage room, he'd only used them a few times for private parties.

"Sydney!"

He'd left her alone too long, dammit. He'd showered in record time, threw on a white shirt, his Sunday blue jeans and black bullhide boots, then hightailed it over here. And still that wasn't fast enough to keep the blasted woman from causing trouble.

Tablecloths and flowers, for God's sake.

"*Sydney!*" He turned and stalked toward the kitchen door. "Where the devil—"

He was going in as she was coming out. The door slammed into his nose with a loud *thwack*. An arrow of hot pain shot straight through his skull, then exploded into thousands of tiny, blinding white stars. His oath was loud and raw.

"Reese Sinclair, what kind of talk is that?" Shaking her head, she moved past him, a small blackboard and easel in her hand, oblivious to the fact she'd just rearranged his septum. "Are you always this cranky in the morning?"

"*Cranky?*" Holding his nose, he followed her to the front door. "You haven't even *begun* to see cranky." His growl was nasally. "But I guarantee you, Syd, it's coming in on a fast-moving train."

She clucked as she slid open the heavy wrought-iron latch on the front door. "Maybe you should have slept in. Lord knows you shouldn't be around people if this is how you behave in the morning."

"If you recall, I *was* sleeping until *you* barged into my bedroom. And what do you mean, *I* shouldn't be around people?" He winced as he gently touched the tender bridge of his nose, then pulled his hand away and checked for blood. Thank goodness there wasn't any. "You're a walking menace to society and *I'm* the one who shouldn't be around people?"

"What in the world are you so excited about?" She set the blackboard on the easel by the hostess podium, then turned to face him. "Why are you holding your nose like that?"

"Tablecloths," he snapped.

"Excuse me?"

"This is a tavern, not a teahouse. We don't use tablecloths."

She frowned at him. "That's why you're holding

your nose? Because you don't like the tablecloths? Heaven's, Reese, even for you, isn't that a bit childish?''

He counted to ten, drew in a slow breath. "No," he ground out between clenched teeth. "You slammed the kitchen door into my nose."

"Oh, dear." She stepped closer and looked up at him. "Let me see."

Protecting his nose with his hand, he backed away. "You've done enough, thank you very much. I'll take my chances with a hematoma."

"Stop being such a baby." She came after him. "I just want to look at it, for Heaven's sake. I won't even touch."

"Yeah, that's what they all say." He held up a hand to warn her off, but she just rolled her eyes at his nonsense and kept coming.

She backed him against the wooden bench for waiting guests, then laid her hands on his shoulders and pushed him down on the seat.

"Now, be still." With her lips pressed firmly together, she placed her hands gently on each side of his jaw and lifted his face. "Hmm. It does look a little red."

"Of course it's red," he complained, but the soft touch of her fingers on his cheeks made the pulsing pain subside. "You clobbered me with the door."

"I'd hardly use the word clobbered." She turned his head to the side, stared at him thoughtfully. "It does look a little crooked, though."

"It was already crooked. Lucian broke it when we were teenagers." Damn, but her fingers felt nice on his face. Her palms were smooth and warm, and she smelled good, too. Like last night. Lavender and something else. He breathed in deeply, concentrated on the familiar scent....

Vanilla. That was it. Sydney smelled like lavender and vanilla. It suited her, he decided.

"Your own brother broke your nose?" She gently touched the sides of his nose with her fingertips, raised her brows when he flinched. "That sounds a little barbaric."

She wore a gold, narrow-band wristwatch and the *tick-tick-tick* echoed in his ears and matched the *thump-thump-thump* in his temple. He couldn't remember a woman's fingers ever being so soft. "He didn't mean to do it. At least, not to me. He was swinging at Callan, who managed to duck the blow. I, unfortunately, was standing directly behind Callan."

Shaking her head with exasperation, she turned his head the other way and stepped between his knees as she leaned in for a closer inspection. "So all those stories I heard about the wild, reckless Sinclairs were true, huh?"

"Bad to the bone, sweetheart. Don't you forget it."

Her lips turned up at that, and he could see the laughter in her eyes. His gaze settled on that sassy mouth of hers and without his approval, his pulse jumped. Damn, but those lips were enticing, turned up slightly at the corners and the upper lip shaped like a cupid's bow. The kind of lips that would be a perfect fit for a man's mouth. And in spite of her sass, he knew she'd taste sweet. Somehow, just knowing that didn't seem to be enough. He had the craziest desire to experience that sweetness.

Something shifted in the air around them. As if an electrical storm were coming; a heaviness that made it hard to breathe. And with him sitting and her standing so close, directly in front of him, between his legs, no less, he became increasingly aware of Sydney as a woman. A woman with curves, very nice curves. He was certain she wasn't aware of it, but her breasts were no more than a handsbreadth from his face. From his mouth.

His heart started slamming around inside his chest like a punching bag. He couldn't be thinking this... *feeling* this way about Sydney. Sydney and sex simply didn't compute. The blow to his nose must have rattled his brain. Except for the fact that he'd already had a fleeting, mildly sexual thought about her earlier in his bedroom. Okay, so maybe the thought was a little more than mild, but it had been fleeting.

And now it was back. With nuclear force.

She moved in closer as she gently touched the bridge of his nose, and his blood began to boil. God help him, he wanted to kiss her. He wanted to slip his fingers under her sweater, feel the warmth of her skin and fill his palms with her soft flesh.

He fisted his hands at his sides and pressed his lips tightly together.

"We should probably put some ice on it," she suggested. There was hesitation in her voice. Uncertainty.

"Probably." But he didn't move, and neither did she. "Does it still hurt?" she asked softly, a little breathlessly.

"Yes." Only it wasn't his nose he was talking about. There was another part of his anatomy that was now throbbing.

"I'm sorry." Her cheeks were flushed, her lips slightly parted, and her hands had moved back to tenderly cup his face. "It does look a little swollen."

He started to choke at her choice of words and she

quickly pulled her hands away and slapped him on the back. "Reese! Are you all right?"

Certain he couldn't speak, he simply nodded, then stood so fast that their bodies collided. Sydney started to fall back, but he grabbed her by the shoulders to steady her.

His hands tightened on her arms as he stared down at her.

Blue eyes wide and soft, she stared up at him.

Damn that mouth of hers.

Damn the torpedoes....

He started to lower his head—

The tavern door swung open wide; Gabe and Melanie came in first, with five-year-old Kevin, Melanie's son, Callan and Abby came next, then Cara and Ian. The noise level in the tavern increased tenfold as his family spilled like a burst dam into the room.

"Hail, hail, the gang's all here!" Gabe scooped a laughing Kevin up in his arms, and Reese saw the lift of Gabe's brows as his gaze landed on the sight of Reese holding Sydney's arms. Reese quickly dropped his hands. Terrific, just terrific. He could only imagine how this must look to everyone. Exactly like what it was, he realized with a silent groan. Good Lord, he'd almost kissed Sydney!

Thank God his family had rescued him from making a mistake like that. Reese knew he'd take some ribbing for it, but that was a small price to pay to be saved from insanity.

"My mom won't let me say hell," Kevin announced to everyone in the way only a five-year-old can. "She gets mad if I even say heck."

"Hail—" Melanie carefully enunciated the word as she pulled a black felt hat from her head, spilling her thick auburn hair around her shoulders "—means hello," she explained. "It also means hail as in pellets of ice, but we can talk about that later. Sydney, how nice to see you."

"Hello, Sydney." Abby smiled sweetly, ran an unconscious hand through the layered golden curls of a new hairdo she wasn't quite used to yet but her husband seemed to love.

"You here for Sunday brunch?" Cara asked, shrugging out of her navy peacoat. Though she had barely begun to show in her pregnancy, her hand instinctively moved to her stomach. Ian, her husband, slipped an arm around her from behind and covered her hand while he pressed his lips to the top of his wife's blond head.

"Sort of." Sydney folded her arms and looked up at Reese with a smug why-don't-you-tell-them expression on her face.

The room was once again quiet, all eyes on him.

Dammit, dammit. He'd never intended for that silly card game to go this far, let alone be standing here trying to explain to his family.

And based on that smirk on Sydney's face, she sure as hell had no intention of making it any easier on him, either.

"Well, it's kind of funny, actually…" He cleared his throat. "See, Sydney and I were playing poker last night—"

That certainly lifted a few eyebrows, but still, no one said anything. "Well, we sort of had a bet, and, uh, I, well, I won." He paused, blurted it out in one quick breath. "So Sydney's going to work here for me for a couple of weeks."

How absolutely ridiculous it sounded to say it out loud. Eight sets of eyes bored into him.

Then all hell broke loose.

"You did *what?*" Cara narrowed her eyes disapprovingly.

"A couple of *weeks?*" Ian's jaw went slack.

"This is a joke, right?" Gabe frowned.

"*Sydney* work *here?*" Callan started to laugh, but Abby elbowed him and shook her head in disbelief.

A pounding started in Reese's head. "I told her I'd waive the deal and cancel all debts. In fact, I even insisted. She refused my offer."

"A deal is a deal," Sydney concurred. "I lost, Reese won. I'm here for two weeks, three hours a day."

"With full pay and tips," Reese added quickly, hoping to redeem himself even a little. It was obvious his brothers thought it was hilarious, while the women all looked at him as if he'd kicked a puppy.

"Isn't your restaurant opening up in a few weeks?" Melanie asked. "How do you have time to be here?"

"I'm pretty much ready to go now, except for the counter that Lucian is installing for me this week," Sydney said. "The next couple of weeks after this one will be just handling details."

"Oooh, look," Abby murmured as she glanced around the room. "Tablecloths and flowers. How pretty everything looks."

"Nice touch, Reese." Cara nodded with approval. "Bringing a little elegance and sophistication to the tavern, are you?"

The tablecloths. Reese had gotten so caught up in his near kiss with Sydney, he'd forgotten about that. The pounding in his head increased. "It was Sydney's idea," he said tightly.

"Reese doesn't like them." Her neck stretched high, Sydney glanced at him. "We were about to discuss it, but we got distracted after I hit him in the nose. On accident, of course.''

Brows went back up again and everyone looked at Reese. He squirmed uncomfortably. "I'm fine," he grumbled.

"Two minutes ago he was howling like a banshee." Sydney shook her head. "You'd have thought I'd tried to murder the man."

The only murder around here, Reese thought irritably, was going to be a long-necked blonde with a gorgeous mouth that wouldn't quit. The sudden image of how he might silence that mouth with his own only made him more irritable.

"Hey, everybody." Lucian burst through the door at that moment. "Please tell me I didn't already miss hearing what happened with our dear baby brother and Sydney Taylor last night. She came storming into the tavern last night mad as a—" He caught sight of Sydney then and stopped abruptly. "Uh, mornin' Syd."

"Morning, Lucian," Sydney said smoothly, then turned a bright smile on the group. "I have a large table by the window up front. Why don't we get you all seated and I'll bring everyone drinks and tell you about today's specials."

Teeth clenched, Reese watched as Sydney, with all the grace and charm of the queen of England, led his family to their table. Good grief, but the woman was infuriating. She wasn't here an hour and she'd taken over. Tablecloths and flowers and—

Today's specials?

He didn't have any today's specials. His gaze shot to the blackboard she'd carried in and set up by the hostess podium.

Crepes Almandine? Quiche Lorraine?

This was an English *tavern,* for God's sake, not some frou-frou French restaurant.

Muttering under his breath, he snatched up the blackboard and easel and headed back to the kitchen. Within the hour, the restaurant would be full, so at the moment, there was no time to "discuss" anything with Sydney.

Something told him that these three hours with Sydney were going to be the longest of his life.

Three hours somehow stretched to four, but with the tavern as busy as it was, Sydney hadn't even noticed she was an hour over her agreed schedule. Apparently Reese hadn't noticed, either, Sydney thought as she slipped into the small employee lounge behind the restrooms, because he hadn't booted her out yet.

With a tired sigh, she sat on the vinyl sofa in the lounge. After losing the poker game last night, she'd tossed and turned all night, then dragged herself out of bed early to get ready for the day. With only two waitresses, plus Reese and herself to see to the customers, she hadn't stopped until now.

The truth be known—and she'd certainly never admit it to Reese—she'd enjoyed every minute of it.

Even as a little girl, Sydney had loved helping out at her mother's endless string of dinner parties and her grandfather's business functions. Whether it was in the kitchen or helping serve in the dining room, she had loved the excitement, the elegant food, the pretty table settings, the flowers, all the wonderful smells and sounds of music and people having a good time.

Sydney had once foolishly told her mother about her dream of opening a small French restaurant in Bloomfield. "Absurd," "waste of time" and "exercise in futility,'' had only been a few of her mother's choice words for the idea.

Sydney had never brought the subject up again, but one year to the day after her mother had died, four weeks after Bobby had left her standing at the altar, Sydney enrolled in culinary school in Paris, bought a ticket for France and never looked back.

She knew people still talked about her behind her back: *Well, is it a surprise?*, they would whisper. *Nobody ever really thought that a handsome jock like Bobby would marry Sydney the Hun. He'd simply felt sorry for her after her mother had died, and after all, her grandfather is the town judge and her family does have loads of money.*

Sydney wasn't stupid. She'd known all that. But she'd really thought that Bobby, even if he hadn't loved her, had cared a little about her, enough that maybe, just maybe she could have a life at least close to what other women had. Husband, children—how desperately she wanted babies!—a little house with a yard.

So maybe she wouldn't have that. But she'd have her restaurant. That was one dream no one could take away from her. Just these few hours this morning in the tavern, showing customers to their tables, taking orders and serving food, had made her feel alive again. She'd felt…needed. And she'd enjoyed every minute. Almost as much as she had enjoyed aggravating Reese.

Closing her eyes, she laid her head back on the sofa and smiled slowly. She knew she was driving him crazy. He'd hated the tablecloths and flowers and had thrown a fit about her additions to the menu. Her smile widened.

Reese Sinclair would rue the day he made that bet with her.

She did feel bad about hitting him in the nose with the door, though. Thank goodness she hadn't broken anything or drawn blood. She didn't believe in physical violence of any kind, and even though it had been an accident, she would have felt terrible if she had seriously hurt him.

But what had happened afterward between them still had her head spinning.

She'd told herself that she'd only touched him because she was concerned he might need medical attention. But when she'd placed her hands on his face she'd had trouble remembering that her inspection was strictly of a clinical nature. His freshly shaved cheeks had felt smooth under her fingertips and the faint scent of his spicy aftershave mesmerized her senses, tempted her to draw his essence more deeply into her lungs. To move closer still.

Had he noticed her hands shaking? Or how difficult it had been for her to breathe? And worst of all—that she'd wanted him to kiss her?

No, she doubted that he had noticed. She'd learned well enough over the years to hide what she was feeling. How else would she have survived an angry, bitter mother who'd never accepted that her husband had left and was never coming back? To the day she'd died, not one thing had ever made her mother happy. Not the family's money or status in the community, not the traveling or fine home they'd lived in. Not even her daughter had ever brought her joy, Sydney thought sadly, though she knew she'd done her best. Her best simply hadn't been good enough.

She wondered if it ever would be.

"What are you still doing here?"

Her eyes flew open at the sound of Reese's voice. He

stood in the lounge doorway, watching her. *Not now,* she thought with a sigh. The last thing she felt like doing at this moment was playing verbal Ping-Pong with Reese Sinclair.

"Even the prisons give five minute breaks, Sinclair." She laid her head back. "I still have one minute left."

"I mean—" he moved into the room and closed the door behind him "—why are you still here at all? Your sentence was up an hour ago."

"I told Julie I'd cover her for a break in ten minutes. She hasn't stopped once in three hours."

"Neither have you. You're going beyond the call of duty here, Syd."

"Well, don't get any ideas that I'm doing it for you," she said, but there was no bite to her words. "I'm just trying to win Julie over so I can steal her away from you. It's not easy to find employees who work that hard."

"It's not easy to find employees, period," he said in agreement. "You have anyone lined up yet?"

She shook her head. "I'm putting an ad in this week."

"Well, if you want long-term, take it from me and stay away from aspiring actors and artists. One day they're here and the next, poof, they magically disappear."

"Sort of like fiancés," she said lightly, then wished she hadn't. She saw the change in Reese's eyes, the pity. More than she hated what people said about her, she hated the pity.

She felt the sofa dip as he sat beside her. Her senses went on immediate alert. She had no idea what was going on with her unexplained feelings toward Reese, but if she'd learned anything this morning, it was to keep as much space between her and him as possible. Especially when she was tired. Tired made her vulnerable, and that was the last thing she wanted to be around Reese. She knew better than to let her guard down with men like Reese Sinclair.

"Sydney." He said her name with such trepidation that she felt her insides wince. "I need to talk to you."

Good grief, if they'd been lovers, she'd have sworn he was getting ready to break it off. But they weren't lovers, of course, and that was a ridiculous thought, anyway.

With a sigh, she sat and leveled her gaze with his. He actually looked worried, she thought in amazement. As if he hated whatever lecture he was about to give her. It had been nice, for two minutes, to have a discussion with Reese without verbal barbs, to talk business as if they were equals. Peers. Only he didn't consider them equals or peers at all, she thought. She knew he considered her restaurant a lark, that she didn't know one little thing about owning a business or the hard work attached to it.

Well, she *did* know what she was doing, and what she didn't know she'd learn. And she'd be damned if she'd sit and cower while he reprimanded her like a child.

"If you're still upset about the flowers and tablecloths, then fine, I won't do that again. I simply thought it might add a certain...*je ne sais quoi*—" she gestured with her hand "—sophistication?"

"That's not what I wanted to—" He stopped, narrowed his eyes. "Sophistication?"

She tucked a stray strand of hair back into the knot on the top of her head. "I wasn't suggesting it for every day. I just thought that a couple of subtle changes would add a little refinement to your Sunday brunch.''

The green of his eyes darkened and a muscle twitched in his jaw. ''You stick that nose of yours up any higher, Syd, you're going to need a guide dog to lead you around.''

''Well, you certainly don't need to be rude.'' She forced her head to remain perfectly level. ''For all it matters to me, you can throw peanut shells on the floor and serve beer in paper cups.''

''Is that so?''

''Yes, that's so.'' She stood, shot a cool gaze at him. ''Well, it's been real, but if you'll excuse me, I'm going to cover for Julie's break before I leave. And I consider this hour overtime, Sinclair. Time-and-a-half.''

*Guide dog,* she fumed as she left the lounge without giving him a chance to respond. She wasn't a snob. And she most certainly did *not* stick her nose up in the—

She tripped over a brass potted plant in the hallway outside the lounge and stumbled forward, barely catching herself. She heard the sound of Reese's chuckle as he watched her from the doorway.

As childish as it was, Sydney wished she had a big fat banana cream pie in her hands. She'd love to rub it in that stupid grin Reese had on his face. Tugging her sweater down, she turned smoothly on her heels and walked away.

# Four

Unless it was a holiday weekend or the height of tourist season, Mondays at the tavern were normally slow so Reese closed and used the time to catch up on errands and the never-ending paperwork that was part of owning his own business. There were always books to be balanced, supplies to be ordered, staff schedules to be juggled and phone calls to be returned. While it was not his favorite part of self-employment, he simply accepted it as a necessary evil, cranked up his favorite Jonny Lang CD and settled down at his desk with a gallon of coffee.

He'd been at it for two hours, and he'd accomplished zip.

All because his mind kept wandering to a completely irascible, highly frustrating, extremely uptight female.

Coffee mug in hand, he leaned back in his desk chair and swiveled around to stare out his office window at the garden he'd had restored after renovating the tavern and inn. In the spring and summer the plants were thick and lush, the flowers a brilliant splash of color, but now, in the fall, the foliage had been cut back and only a few hardy chrysanthemums and asters still bloomed. While Jonny's gravelly voice wailed about lies and sex, Reese watched a bumblebee explore one budding branch of Winter Heath and, for the hundredth time, his mind drifted to Sydney.

After only one day the situation had already gotten out of hand. When he'd gone to the employee's lounge yesterday, he'd had every intention of putting an end to this farce. She'd looked so tired sitting on the couch with her head back and her eyes closed. So guileless. Soft and serene.

Quiet.

He smiled at that thought. He'd certainly never admit it to anyone, but he was not only getting used to that sass of hers, he actually enjoyed it. She said what was on her mind, and even though he didn't always like it, he had to at least respect her honesty. She didn't use her femininity to get her way or manipulate. No games of seduction or flirtation. No pouting or sulking. Even when she'd had to wipe down tables or sweep up a spilled bottle of catsup, she simply applied herself to the task without hesitation.

Somehow he'd never pictured Sydney Taylor doing anything as menial as taking drink orders or clearing dishes. She'd been born with a silver spoon in that enticing mouth of hers, and he doubted she'd ever lifted a finger for anything more strenuous than a manicure.

But she certainly had yesterday morning. She'd run her cute little behind off and never once complained. If he hadn't known better, he would have sworn she'd actually *enjoyed* working. Other than those damn table-cloths and the admonishment she'd given George Hubbel for ordering the double pork sausage skillet breakfast with extra cheese—George had just been released from the hospital following a triple bypass—the morning had gone by great.

Then she'd just had to go and get all snooty on him again. Implying the tavern lacked "sophistication." It was a tavern, for crying out loud. Not Antoines. If he let her have her way, she probably would have put out finger bowls and chilled salad forks. To Reese, chilled salad forks were the epitome of nothingness.

So he'd been compelled to continue their little parody. Just for another day or two, he told himself. That ought to be long enough to make Sydney Taylor throw in the towel.

He was a man with a plan.

Smiling, he took a sip of coffee, watching as the bumblebee stumbled out of the Winter Heath like a drunken sailor, then flew off. Sydney just needed a little instruction on how to relax and not be so serious all the time, Reese told himself. Not to be so high-and-mighty.

To think he'd almost kissed her. He snorted at the thought, then frowned.

He *still* wanted to kiss her.

Dammit, what was it about the woman that had him thinking about her when he needed to be working? He'd never thought about Sydney like that before. Never noticed how smooth her skin was, or how soft the blue of her eyes was, how incredibly tantalizing her mouth was. And when she'd stepped between his legs and moved so close, her breasts only inches away from him, he could have simply leaned forward and—

"Yo, Reese, you in here?"

He jumped at the sound of Lucian's voice, swore when coffee spilled over the sides of the cup in his hand and stained the front of the blue denim shirt he had on. He was still swearing as Lucian plopped himself down in a chair on the opposite side of the desk.

When Reese swiveled his chair around, Lucian took in the wet spot on his brother's shirt and lifted his brow. "Been drinking long?"

Reese narrowed his eyes. "Been sneaking up on people long?"

"I didn't sneak. You were in a galaxy far, far away, or at least your mind was." Lucian stretched his long legs out in front of him and settled back comfortably. "So what's her name?"

"Whose name?" Reese swiped at the front of his shirt, rummaged through the paperwork on his desk looking for a napkin, found one underneath his quarterly federal tax form.

"Whoever you were lusting over when I came in. I know the look, Bro. So who is it? Susan Williams? I heard she and Larry split up."

"They split up once a week. I'm trying to work here, Lucian. Get lost."

Undaunted, Lucian dug in like a dog after a bone. "It's Nancy Turlow, isn't it? She came into the tavern last Saturday with Heather and couldn't take her eyes off you."

Reese clenched his jaw, then picked up a pencil and turned his attention back to the ledger on his desk. "If the construction business is so slow you've got nothing better to do than sit around and speculate on my love life," he said dryly, "I've got some cracked tile in one of the guest rooms. Work me up an estimate and get back to me tomorrow."

"Gosh, thanks," Lucian said flatly. "As soon as we finish the strip mall we're building over in Ridgeway, then the four-story office building in Angel City, I'll get right on that. But for the record, I am here on business. I'm looking for Sydney."

"Sydney?" His head came up. "What do you want with Sydney?"

"Gabe asked me to stop by her place and take measurements on the countertop she ordered from him. She wasn't there, so I thought she might be here."

"Do you see her here?"

"Nope. But since you won her in that poker game, I just thought—"

"I didn't win *her*, dammit." Reese pushed away from his desk and stalked to the window. He stared out into the garden, frowned at the sight of Boomer sunning himself on the soft leaves of a lamb's ear plant. He shook his head, then sighed. "How the hell was I to know that she really knew how to play poker?"

Lucian stared thoughtfully at his brother for a long time, then slowly raised his brows. "You cheated."

"What?" Reese turned sharply.

"You cheated." Lucian leaned back in his chair. "I know you, Bro. You can call a good bluff, but you can't lie to me. It's right there in your eyes. You cheated."

Reese shoved his hands into the front pockets of his jeans. "She was winning. And she was so damn smug about it. She just needed to be taken down a peg or two."

"And you, of course, were the man to do it?"

He shrugged. "I never expected her to go through with it. It was...a joke."

"Doesn't look like you're laughing," Lucian noted.

"I tried to call it off, especially yesterday, after she'd

worked so hard here at the tavern. I was even going to confess. Then she stuck that pretty little nose of hers up in the air again and for some reason, I just couldn't let it go."

Lucian chuckled softly. "Well, I'll be damned. That's lust in your eyes, Bro. Who would have ever believed you'd be hot for *Sydney?*"

Reese made a rude sound. "Even coming from you, Lucian, that's about the stupidest thing I've ever heard. I am not remotely interested in Sydney that way."

Reese's head went up at a sound from the hallway outside his office, then he relaxed when Marilyn, one of his night-shift waitresses poked her head in the door and smiled. "Hey, boss, can I pick up my check now?" Her gaze slid to Lucian and her smile turned provocative. "Hi, Lucian."

"Hey, Mar." Lucian easily slipped into charm mode. "What's up?"

Reese found the woman's paycheck on his desk while she and Lucian bantered back and forth, then quickly hustled her out.

"Look, I know I got carried away." Reese dragged a hand through his hair. "And believe me, I'm paying for it big time. But as far as there being anything between Sydney and me, that's just completely—"

"Knock, knock. Little sister's here."

Reese groaned as Cara came waltzing into his office, her pink skirt swirling around her legs and her arms loaded with shopping bags. He might as well have a revolving door on his office the way people were coming in and out.

"What about Sydney?" Cara asked.

"Reese has a thing for her." Lucian rose, took the bags from his sister's arms.

Cara hesitated, looked at Reese. "You have a thing for Sydney?"

Why the hell couldn't he have been an only child? he thought irritably. "I do *not* have a thing for Sydney," he snapped. "Doesn't anyone in my family work anymore?"

"Not on Mondays." Cara brushed her blond hair back with her fingers and sat in the chair Lucian had occupied. She'd once been a private investigator, but now she ran a women's shelter in Philadelphia founded by her husband's grandmother. "I brought decorations for the surprise party we're throwing here for Gabe and Melanie on Saturday."

"What surprise party?" Since it was off the subject of Sydney, Reese eagerly pursued his sister's announcement.

"We never celebrated their engagement, so Abby and I thought we'd give them a surprise dinner party here." Cara slipped her flats off her feet and frowned at her swollen feet. "Good Heavens, at this rate, my feet will be the size of shoe boxes by the time this baby's born."

"They're getting married in a month," Lucian said, setting her bags down beside the desk. "What do they need a party for now?"

"Men." Cara sighed and shook her head. "Of course we have to give them a party."

Confused, Reese and Lucian looked at each other and shrugged.

"Just family." Cara stretched her feet and wiggled her toes. "Something nice, but not fancy. I'll work up a menu with Corky."

"Work up a menu?" Reese frowned. "What's wrong with the menu I've already got?"

"There's nothing *wrong* with your menu," Cara said

with all the patience of a kindergarten teacher. "Abby and I just think we should do something special. Now what's this about you and Sydney?"

Reese groaned silently. He should have known she'd come back around to the one subject he didn't want to talk about. "There is *nothing* about me and Sydney. She's just…helping out here while I'm shorthanded. We explained all that yesterday. I tried to let her out of the agreement, but she's stubborn as a mule."

"Honorable is a better word," Cara said and stared at him thoughtfully. "And if you had lost this *bet* you'd made, then what?"

Dammit, Reese fumed. Big families were like small towns, only worse. They wanted to know every little teeny tiny detail of their sibling's life, whether it was their business or not. But it was one thing for Lucian to know that he'd cheated in the poker game with Sydney, and quite another if his sister found out. She'd have him drawn and quartered.

Well, she didn't need to find out. No one needed to find out, for that matter. Lucian might razz him endlessly in private, but he wouldn't tell Cara or anyone else, Reese was certain of that.

He just needed to act casual. Nonchalant. He picked up his pencil and entered gibberish in one of the columns. "I would have had to lock Boomer up so he'd stop digging up her flowers."

"What kind of a deal is that?" Cara stared at him in amazement. "You *should* keep him fenced in anyway, deal or no deal." Cara shook her head. "Sydney's smarter than to bet something as simple as that. What are you holding back, Reese?"

He kept his eyes glued to the page in front of him as

if it were a fascinating novel. "I'd have to work at her place for two weeks," he mumbled quickly.

Now it was Lucian and Cara's turn to stare at each other in wide-eyed amazement. When they both began to laugh, Reese slammed his pencil down. "What's so damn funny?"

"You—" Lucian's shoulders were shaking "—you work for Sydney Taylor in her French restaurant? I'd eat a whole plate of those slimy little cooked snails to see that."

"How 'bout you eat my fist instead?" Reese rose stiffly and glared at his brother.

"No violence in the presence of a pregnant lady," Cara warned, struggling to contain her mirth. "Now, Reese, you've got to admit it, if you'd lost, it would have been pretty funny."

Yeah, gut-splitting, he thought and sat back down in a huff. "Why don't you both take a hike? I've got better things to do than sit around thinking about Sydney all day."

Cara went still, and even Lucian stopped laughing long enough to stare at him. "*Thinking* about Sydney?" Cara asked, raising her brow.

Dammit, *dammit*. "Talking. I said *talking*."

"No, you didn't. You said thinking," Lucian said. "Well, well. So you and Sydney *do* have a thing for each other."

"*I do not have a thing for Sydney,*" he boomed.

"Of course he doesn't."

All heads turned at the sound of Sydney's voice coming from the doorway. She stood there, wearing a simple white silk, scoop-necked blouse and a calf-length, dark blue silk skirt. There was a long moment of strained silence as Sydney's ice-blue eyes met Reese's, then she moved as gracefully across the room as if she were performing *Swan Lake*.

"Hey, Syd." Lucian cleared his throat. "Ah, I was looking for you."

She turned those incredible eyes on Lucian. "Oh?"

"Yeah, ah, Gabe asked me to take some measurements for the countertop you ordered."

She reached into her skirt pocket and pulled out a set of keys. "You can leave them inside when you're finished. I have a duplicate set."

Grasping at the opportunity to escape, Lucian snatched up the keys. "Well, I'll just get to those measurements, then."

"Could you give me a hand with these packages, Lucian?" Cara quickly slipped her shoes back on and stood. "Just leave the two blue bags. They're for the party. Nice to see you again, Sydney," Cara said as she and Lucian moved toward the door. "Please give my best to your grandfather, will you?"

"Certainly." Sydney kept her gaze directly on Reese.

*Cowards.* Reese frowned after his brother and sister when they disappeared from the room. When he wanted them to leave they wouldn't. Now he wanted them to stay and they couldn't get out of here fast enough.

"Hey, Syd." He turned his attention to the woman who stood watching him, her arms folded primly across her chest. Unknowingly, the gesture lifted and pressed her breasts firmly upward. *Don't think about her breasts,* he told himself, but the more he told himself not to think about them, and certainly not to look, the more he wanted to.

"Where in the world would Lucian get such a preposterous idea that either one of us would have a *thing* for the other?" Sydney asked.

"Didn't you know that Lucian was dropped on his head when he was a baby?" Reese said easily and slipped back into his desk chair.

"Is that so?" She arched one delicate brow.

"God's truth." He raised his hand to emphasize the veracity of his statement. At the same time, he forced his gaze to stay steady with hers, but it felt like a fish on the end of a line, tugging and pulling, trying to draw his attention down to the neckline of her blouse. "My parents thought about an institution when it became apparent there was permanent damage, but since he wasn't dangerous, they kept him at home."

"Every Sinclair man is dangerous," Sydney said, shaking her head. "You should all come with a warning label that says you're hazardous to the female sex."

"I love it when you talk dirty," Reese said huskily. And even though he was teasing, the sudden image of pillow talk with Sydney did make his pulse race.

*Keep your eyes on her face,* he repeated over and over, though he desperately wanted to slide a long, slow look over those lovely breasts, then down her silk-covered slender hips. What was she wearing underneath? he wondered, then gave himself a mental shake and decided he was the one with brain damage.

"Reese Sinclair." Sydney shook her head and sighed. "Can't you be serious for even one minute? It's ludicrous to think that you would have feelings for me or that I would have feelings for you that were of a physical nature. I just don't want your family getting the wrong idea about us."

Her words had *snob* written all over them, Reese thought with annoyance. And just why was it so ludicrous for her to have any feelings for him that were of a "physical nature"? What the hell was wrong with him? *She* was the one walking around as if she had too much starch in her collar.

Just once, he'd like to shake that ivory tower she lived in. He stood slowly, moved toward her with intent. "What's wrong with physical, Syd? I happen to like physical. In fact, I'm feeling extremely physical at this very moment."

"I hear lifting weights is quite an effective release of energy."

"There are other ways to release energy that are a lot more enjoyable," he murmured, moving closer. His gaze dropped to her mouth, and though he had no intention of this going anywhere, the jolt of desire that shot to his groin obviously had a mind of its own.

"Tennis is an excellent form of exercise," she suggested.

Wary, Sydney watched Reese approach, but refused to back away. Refused to think about those large hands of his, that long, muscular body and broad shoulders. She forced herself to think about a brandy sauce she'd been experimenting with, if it had enough butter, maybe a little less brown sugar. Vanilla, she decided, she'd add a little extra vanilla.

"Never could really get into the game myself." Reese moved past her and closed the office door.

Sydney's insides immediately formed a conga line from her head to her toes. "Is that so?" she said, forcing a bored tone to her voice, when she was anything but.

He smiled, then came up behind her, touched the back of her neck with his fingertip. "I prefer contact sports myself. Something that works the circulatory system and strengthens muscle tone. Something that really gets the heart pumping."

Her heart *was* pumping furiously. It was one thing to exchange verbal banter with him, but this was something entirely different. Something much more… sensual. She knew that Reese was teasing her, and as much as it aggravated her, it also excited her.

He wanted her to put a stop to his nonsense, expected her to. This was a game to Reese, she realized. He was certain she would yell "uncle" first. He was counting on it. He wasn't interested in her that way. And she, of course, wasn't interested in him that way, either.

Well, he started it, she thought with annoyance. Let *him* be the one to finish it. In spite of herself, she shivered when he slid the tip of his finger over the bare skin on her neck.

"Did anyone ever tell you that you have a pretty neck? And hair, too." Her breath caught when he moved behind her and brought his mouth closer to her ear. "Do you ever let your hair down, Syd?"

The warmth of his breath on her neck and ear sent ripples of pleasure over her skin. Every warning system screamed at her to run, to get away as fast as she could, but she knew that was what he wanted. He'd know then that he'd won, that he was irresistible to even cold-as-ice Sydney Taylor. And if that ego of his got any bigger, Reese Sinclair wouldn't even be able to walk through a doorway.

"Of course I let my hair down," she said calmly, ignoring the dull, heavy thud of her heart against her ribs. "When I wash it, before I go to bed, when I go to the beauty salon for a trim, or there's this wonderful oil pack that—"

"I'd like to see it," he said, skimming two fingertips up her neck.

Sydney realized she wasn't breathing and forced herself to draw in air. "Well, if you really want to. It's highly irregular, but I'm sure I could arrange it with my stylist. They pour about a cup of hot oil over wet hair, put a shower cap on your head, then stick you under the dryer for about—"

"Your hair down, Syd," he interrupted. "I'd like to see you let your hair down."

She'd had no idea how sensitive the skin on her neck was. Reese's touch was light as a feather, yet it packed the punch of a boxer. As ridiculous as it seemed, her knees were actually *weak,* her pulse was racing and she felt…hot. Very hot.

"Do you mean that figuratively, or literally?" she asked, then winced at the breathless sound she heard in her voice.

"Both." He moved closer still, brought his mouth within a whisper of her ear. She shuddered, was furious that she couldn't stop it and that Reese must have seen, too.

What made her even more furious was that she liked it. What he was doing to her, the way she felt. She liked it a lot. Wanted him to keep doing exactly what he was doing, wanted to keep feeling exactly as she was feeling.

She struggled to breathe, struggled to remain composed and collected when she really wanted to run. Into his arms or for the door, she wasn't sure which. But if he kept looking at her the way he was, if he kept touching her, she was going to find out real soon.

A knock at the door made her jump.

"Delivery." The door opened, and a young man with bleached white hair and double nose rings stuck his head in. "Hey, Reese, you wanna show me where you want all these bags?"

Reese gave Sydney one short, intense look, then brushed past her and followed the other man into the tavern. The breath she'd been holding shuddered out and she stumbled over to the desk to steady herself. That was close. Much too close. She'd nearly thrown herself in his arms and begged him to kiss her. Talk about pathetic, she thought with disgust. If she wanted to kiss anybody, it should be that delivery man for interrupting.

But just once, she thought, just once she wished a man would say things like that to her, that she had pretty hair or a nice neck, and he would mean them. *Really* mean them. It wouldn't be a game, like with Reese, or a lie, like Bobby. Just once she wished someone would say sweet things to her and it would be sincere.

She sighed, then drew in a long, slow breath and followed Reese out into the tavern. He was signing for the delivery and joking with the young man—Jessie— about the multitude of piercings on his body.

Sydney waited for the deliveryman to leave, then cautiously made her way toward Reese, who was staring intently at a four-foot-high pile of large produce bags.

Maybe she should try to get along with him, she thought. There was no reason for the two of them to argue or constantly snipe at each other. Maybe he was right. Maybe she should let her hair down, just a little.

What if maybe, just maybe, he *had* actually felt something when he'd been teasing her?

She moved beside him, ready to be pleasant and agreeable, even if it killed her. He turned when he saw her, looked at her with an expression that could only be described as sheer joy.

She smiled back and relaxed a little. "Reese—"

"Ah, there you are," he said, grinning. "This might take a while, so you better get started."

"Take a while?" she repeated dumbly.

He slapped a hand on top of the bags. "I thought it was a great idea you had, sort of give the tavern a rustic ambiance."

"What on earth are you talking about?" She stared at him in confusion, then looked at the bags under his hand.

Peanuts. Bags and bags of peanuts. Hundreds and *thousands* of peanuts.

"You can start shelling these for the floor and throw the nuts into a container. We'll serve them at the bar."

She stared at him, blinked. "This is a joke, right?"

"No joke," he said easily. Gone was the dangerous, sexual predator she'd nearly thrown herself at. Frivolous, life-is-a-game Reese Sinclair was back.

"You really expect me to shell all these nuts? By hand?"

"Don't know any other way to do it, and since it was your idea, I figured you'd want to be in charge."

What a fool she'd been to let her guard down with this man! An idiot. Well, it wouldn't happen again. Folding her arms, she lifted her chin and pointed it at him. "This isn't nearly enough peanuts to evenly distribute and create the proper illusion of 'rustic' as you called it. If you're going to do something, Reese, you should at least do it right."

He cocked one brow and gave her his most charming smile. "Well, Syd, I'm sure I can trust you to handle this project all on your own. You have carte blanche, sweetheart, and since you're only here three hours, I suggest you get started right away. This is a whole lotta nuts."

Whistling, he snatched up his truck keys from the bar counter, then left her in the tavern, alone.

Sydney hurried across the tavern and stared out the front window, watched Reese get into his truck and drive off.

The nerve of him! It would take her hours to shell all these nuts. Days. She knew that wasn't really what he wanted. He was making a point here, hoping she'd back down. Give up. Throw in the towel.

Well, Sydney Taylor didn't give up. Not by a long shot.

Across the street, she saw Lucian come out of the front door of her building and head back toward the tavern. He stopped in the parking lot to talk to Jessie the Peanut Boy, who was standing inside the back of his delivery truck, moving bags of peanuts.

She watched the two men for a moment, then glanced back over her shoulder at the mountain of nuts she'd been left to shell.

A smile spread slowly across her face.

Shoulders squared, chin up, she went out to the parking lot.

# Five

Reese stayed away from the tavern for the next two hours and fifteen minutes. He'd had several errands to run: the bank, Harry's Hardware, Sav-More Stationery, the post office, and garden center. He disliked errands as much as he disliked paperwork, but today he'd actually had a smile on his face as he'd strolled through the aisles of the stores and waited in line at the bank. Several times, to the confusion of anyone standing close to him, he'd even started laughing out loud.

The stunned look on Sydney's face when he'd told her she had to shell all those peanuts—Lord, it was priceless. He'd cherish that moment forever.

That oughta take a little starch out of that high-and-mighty collar of hers, he thought as he pulled his truck into a space in the front parking lot of the tavern. And a little lesson in humility certainly never hurt anyone.

He would have loved to stick around and watch her

shell peanut after endless peanut, but after their little…encounter…in his office earlier, he had thought it best to keep his distance from her for a while. He seemed to be having continuous lapses of sanity when it came to the woman.

He'd never admit it to a living soul, but Sydney Taylor made him nervous.

Women never made him nervous. He loved the female gender and everything about them: their mysteries and idiosyncrasies, the way they smelled, the way they moved. The curve of their legs and the sway of their hips. He'd always been comfortable with the opposite sex. Completely in control. If he was attracted to a woman, and she was attracted to him, it had always been easy to take it to the next step. He certainly didn't sleep with every woman that he dated, but he always enjoyed their company.

Simple and uncomplicated, that had always been his motto.

Then along came Sydney.

Sydney was anything but simple and uncomplicated. She was bullheaded, snooty, condescending and wound up tight as a new Swiss watch. No female had ever gotten under his skin the way Sydney had. He'd never spent hours thinking about any one particular woman, gnashing his teeth in exasperation one minute, then the next, fantasizing about the soft curve of her neck and what it would taste like, what it would feel like under his hands and mouth.

And earlier, when he had touched that lovely neck, he'd wanted to do a hell of a lot more than fantasize. He'd felt her shudder under his touch, and he knew that she wasn't so disinterested, wasn't so cool, as she'd have him believe. He could have kissed her right then—

he'd certainly wanted to—and she would have let him. It wouldn't have been a big deal. He'd kissed lots of women, for crying out loud, and while it might have been mutually pleasant, it hadn't really meant anything beyond that. Just a kiss.

So why, then, hadn't he just done it?

Why had he held back, been relieved, even, when Jessie had interrupted them?

And the biggest question of all: Why hadn't he ended this charade? Told her the truth and taken his lumps?

Pride. That's what it was. Every time Sydney looked down at him, every time she sniffed and lifted that little chin of hers, he couldn't let it go. He wanted her to surrender. To give up. It was that simple. And stupid, he admitted to himself.

Well, Ms. Sydney Taylor should be sufficiently humbled by now, he thought, climbing out of his truck and heading for the tavern entrance. He could only imagine the snit she would be in after two hours of shelling peanuts.

He grinned at the thought.

He found her sitting at the bar, perched primly on a barstool, her back to him. On the floor beside her was a cardboard box she'd tossed the empty shells into. To her right, on the counter, was a large bowl half-filled with shelled peanuts.

He shouldn't rub it in, he thought gleefully. There was certainly no need to rile her anymore than he already had.

Yeah, right. Not in a million years would he let an opportunity to ruffle Sydney Taylor's feathers pass him by.

Whistling cheerfully, he strode into the tavern right

up to her. "Hey, Syd, that's a whole bunch of nuts you got there. Looks like you've been a busy girl."

"'Idleness is only the refuge of weak minds,'" she said, blithely quoting Chesterfield.

He leaned close. "'Beauty stands in the admiration only of weak minds led captive,'" he quoted right back at her.

Astonishment widened her eyes. "You know Milton?"

"English Lit 102. Professor Lori Hunter. A hot babe I wanted to impress with my term paper."

Sydney arched one brow. "And did you?"

He grinned at her. "I got an A."

"I'm sure."

She turned her attention back to her task and he watched her quickly snap and shell the peanuts inside. She had long, slender, delicate hands and he remembered the touch of her fingers on his face the other day. Smooth and soft. Warm. *Don't go there, Reese,* he reminded himself.

"You've got a natural talent there, Syd," he said, forcing his mind back to his intention to ruffle her feathers, not stroke them.

"It's easy once you get into the rhythm." She didn't even glance at him, just dropped the empty shell into the box at her feet and reached for another peanut. "It's actually quite relaxing. Sort of like needlepoint or knitting."

Relaxing? Like needlepoint? Sure it was, he thought, holding back his grin. She was convincing, all right, but he knew she was bluffing. Trying to get his goat. *Not gonna work, Syd.*

"Shall I order more?" he suggested. "You didn't think there would be enough earlier."

"Won't be necessary." She looked up and smiled sweetly at him.

Ha. He didn't think so. But her smile captivated him, drew his attention to her mouth. She wasn't wearing lipstick, but still her lips were rosy. He quickly snapped his gaze back to hers. Which didn't help much. Her blue eyes were sparkling with pleasure.

*Not this time, Sydney,* he thought with smug satisfaction. No way was she going to distract him. He had no doubt that, inside, Sydney was seething mad. He intended to relish every moment of his conquest. Another ten pounds of peanuts and she'd cave. He was certain of it.

He couldn't wait.

"Well, Syd, it's been nice chatting with you. If you need anything—" *like a white flag or a towel* "—I'll be in my office."

She waved a hand, then turned back to the bar and continued diligently with her task.

He had to hand it to her, Reese thought as he headed for his office. She was putting up a really good front. If he didn't know better, he'd think she was actually having a good time. Which, of course, she wasn't. Chuckling to himself, he opened his office door.

"What the—"

An avalanche of peanuts flowed from his office.

Thousands, *millions* of peanuts consumed him, swept him up in a torrent and carried him along. He struggled to gain his ground, then went down and under, cursing and sputtering. Like lava flow, they kept coming, spilling into the narrow hallway outside his office and scattering across the hardwood floor.

When at last it stopped, he lay there, flat on his back,

staring up at the ceiling, wearing a blanket of peanuts. He narrowed his eyes.

Somebody was going to die.

When that somebody leaned over him, he stared up at her.

"I guess I forgot to mention I ordered a few more bags of peanuts." She raised her brows in mock concern. "You did say I should handle it, and since I wasn't sure where to put them I went ahead and—"

Sydney squeaked when Reese's hand snaked out and grabbed her down and on top of him. In one swift, fluid move, he rolled and had her pinned underneath him. Peanuts crunched and crumbled. Eyes wide, mouth still open, she looked up at him, saw the murderous glint in his eyes.

And the broken bits of peanut shells covering his head and clothes.

She couldn't help it. She started to laugh.

A muscle jumped in Reese's temple as he stared down at her. Revenge glistened in his deep green eyes. A slow, sinister smile touched his mouth.

Uh-oh.

Sydney struggled to stand, but Reese would have no part of it. He straddled her, then scooped up handfuls of peanuts and dumped them on her.

A peanut war ensued.

Lying on her back with Reese towering over her, Sydney had the disadvantage, but she held her own. Peanuts flew like popping corn. Sydney shrieked, ducked one large armful he attempted to throw on her, then scooped up two handfuls and flung them at him. They were both spitting out salty chunks of peanut shells, laughing and thrashing around on a thick, crunchy blanket of peanuts.

She snatched up another handful, but he grabbed her wrists and held her arms at her sides. She tried to break free, but his grip only tightened. He was much too strong to throw him off, and she knew she would only embarrass herself if she tried.

"Had enough?" she asked breathlessly.

He raised his brow at the absurdity of her question. Considering the current circumstances, she was hardly in a position to ask him that.

Reese shook his head and fragments of peanut shell floated down from his hair. "You want to tell me—" he drew in a deep lungful of air "—how you managed this little trick by yourself?"

"Lucian helped." She knew her smile was smug, but she didn't care. "We climbed in your office window, emptied all the bags from the delivery truck. Jessie helped, too, he's such a sweetheart—and then we went out the window again."

"My brother, my own flesh and blood, was part of this evil plot? And Jessie, too?" Reese's dark frown didn't make it to his eyes. "A triple murder in Bloomfield County. This will definitely be breaking news on the television tonight."

Her smile widened. "Lucian wanted to stick around for the show, but he had an appointment."

"Is that so?"

Reese's breathing had eased, but her chest still rose and fell sharply as she struggled for air. As he stared down at her, Sydney felt an imperceptible shift in the mood. She became increasingly aware of the fact that Reese was straddling her body. His large hands circled her wrists and held her captive.

Her heart skipped, then started to race. She blew a strand of loose hair from her eyes, reminded herself that they were simply having a little fun; it didn't mean anything.

But his body lying on top of hers was so intimate, so *sexual*....

"I—I'm supposed to give a detailed report to him later." She told herself that the breathless quality to her voice was merely a result of her struggling to escape, but at a very deep, instinctive level she knew it was much more than that.

"I'll give him a report," Reese said. "Right after he picks his teeth out of his tonsils."

"I claim full responsibility for my actions," she said emphatically. "I insist that all consequences be directed at me."

"You insist, do you?" His voice turned husky. "All consequences? You sure about that, Syd?"

She wasn't sure about anything at the moment. In fact, she was finding it difficult to think at all. She'd never been more aware of a man in her entire life. Reese's body was long and hard and muscular. The angles of his face were sharp now, his jaw clenched, his eyes narrowed and dancing with the devil. His strong mouth was pressed into a smirk, his dark hair tousled, dusted with flecks of peanut shells. A vein pulsed at the base of his throat, and for the life of her, she couldn't take her eyes off that spot.

The air shimmered around them. Grew taut.

She didn't want this. Didn't want to cross over any lines that she'd regret. She had enough regrets in her life at the moment, and she had no intention of adding Reese Sinclair to that list.

The pulsing in her body screamed at her to shut up and offer herself to Reese without question or protest.

Thank Heavens she still had a thread of good judgment left.

"So," she said lightly, desperately wanting to pull the mood back to playful instead of the dark, sensual tone that had suddenly closed in around them. "Had enough, Sinclair?"

He stared at her for a long moment, then his gaze dropped to her mouth. "Not even close, Syd," he said, his voice strained.

Her body still pinned underneath his, he lifted her arms over her head, then lowered his mouth to hers. At the first light touch of his lips on hers, she held very still, determined not to respond.

And then that last thread of good judgment she'd been so proud of snapped like a twig in a tornado.

His mouth was firm and strong, his lips gentle. Her heart slammed in her chest as he nibbled on the corner of her lips. Liquid heat rushed through her body; her skin felt tight and tingly.

"Reese," she whispered, her lips moving against his, "I don't think—"

"Me, either."

Then he completely destroyed her.

He crushed his mouth to hers. Her senses spun at the fierce demand of his lips, the press of his strong body over hers, the faint masculine scent that was Reese. She'd heard all those silly myths of bone-melting, exploding fireworks kisses, but she'd never believed in them. They simply had been romantic fairy tales and legends.

They were true.

She had no defenses against this, against him. His kiss stripped away every argument, every last remnant of reason and logic. Her mind was no longer in control; she could only feel.

And it felt wonderful.

He deepened the kiss, and a low, desperate moan rose from deep in her throat. She squirmed underneath him, frustrated that he still held her arms, yet excited at the same time. Intense pleasure sparked in her blood, then burst into flames. When his hands finally released her wrists, then slid down her arms, she trembled in anticipation.

Needing him closer, she wound her arms tightly around his neck. His mouth moved down her throat, his tongue, hot and wet, tasted and nipped. He murmured something against her ear and his warm breath sent ripples of delight through her. Skillfully he moved his hands down her sides, then lower still, gathering her skirt upward, exposing her calves, then her thighs. His callused hands were rough on her sensitive skin. She shivered at his touch. An ache settled between her legs, and she moved restlessly against him, wanting more.

Then his hands moved upward and slid under her blouse.

She gasped when he cupped her breasts, arched upward when his thumbs caressed her hardened nipples.

He nipped at the base of her throat, murmured her name, then moved lower....

"Hello! Anybody here?"

Both she and Reese jumped at the deep, booming voice that echoed from the empty tavern into the hallway where they lay on the floor, practically making love.

Muttering an oath, Reese moved off of her, then stood, reached out a hand to help her up. Shaking, she rose on watery knees, quickly smoothed her skirt and blouse.

"Sydney Marie Taylor!" the voice bellowed again. "Are you here, girl?"

She swallowed back the panic in her throat, then straightened her shoulders. Reese looked at her, his mouth pressed into a thin, hard line.

She sucked in a deep breath and called out, "In here, Grandfather."

# Six

Judge Randolph "Duffy" Tremaine Howland, Bloomfield County's most prominent and most wealthy citizen, stood at the end of the hallway leading to Reese's office. His three-piece steel-gray suit matched the color of his keen eyes. Eyes now narrowed sharply as he took in the peanuts on the floor and the disheveled state of his granddaughter's and Reese's clothing.

Reese gritted his teeth and held back the groan in his throat. Dammit, dammit, dammit.

"Hello, Judge Howland." Reese nodded casually, though he felt anything *but* casual at the moment. His body still tight with need, his blood still simmering, it was all he could do not to snatch Sydney back into his arms, drag her into his office, then shut the door to finish what they'd started. To hell with her grandfather or anyone who dared interrupt them.

But as reality slowly crept into his dazed brain, as he

looked at the judge, then Sydney, with her flushed cheeks and tousled hair, he knew without a doubt that was *not* going to happen.

Duffy's gaze shot from Sydney to Reese, then dropped to the floor and the carpet of peanuts. "What on God's good earth is going on here?" the elderly man boomed.

Sydney smoothed her hands over the front of her skirt, then cleared her throat. "We were just, ah, cleaning up a bag of peanuts that spilled. Weren't we, Reese?"

Oh, yeah. Everyone cleans up spilled peanuts by thrashing around on the floor in a lip lock, Reese thought. "Right. Spilled peanuts," he muttered.

The judge's eyes narrowed as he studied them both. His mouth pressed into a thin line, Duffy raised one thick, silver brow and leveled a stern gaze at his granddaughter. "Sydney, if you needed money, why didn't you come to me?"

"If I needed money?" Sydney frowned, obviously confused by the sudden shift of conversation. "I don't need any money."

"Then why are you working here—in a tavern, of all places, if you don't need money?"

Reese crossed his arms and leaned back against the doorjamb. *Yeah, Syd, go ahead and tell your grandfather why you're working here....*

Sydney folded her hands primly in front of her. The pose was truly noble, but Reese thought that the empty peanut shell dangling from her hair spoiled the effect.

"I would hardly describe my position here as *working*, Grandfather," she said, her tone as regal as her demeanor.

"I was informed you were cleaning tables and serving food here yesterday." Duffy drew his thick silver brows together. "What would you call that?"

She started to nibble on her bottom lip. "Well...it's not, it's more like—" She hesitated.

"Spit it out, girl," Duffy barked.

"It's more like a...business arrangement," she said carefully. "I'm helping Reese out for a few days while he's shorthanded and—"

She paused, looked at Reese for back-up. He grinned at her. *Sorry, Syd. You're on your own.* As if she heard his thoughts, her lips pressed into a thin line.

She turned back to her grandfather. "And in exchange he's, ah, consulting with me. Giving me his expert advice on the efficient management of a restaurant."

"Is that so?" Duffy narrowed a dubious gaze at Reese. "Why would you advise the competition?"

Reese glanced at Sydney, considered giving her a break, then thought of all the peanuts he'd be cleaning up for weeks, probably months, to come. And besides, he couldn't possibly let this opportunity pass him by. In spite of that mind-boggling kiss they'd just shared, in spite of the fact he wanted to kiss her again, and more, he and Sydney were, after all, still adversaries.

"Well, sir, in all honesty, when Sydney first came to me, asking for my help, I have to admit that I did turn her down." Reese shook his head and sighed. "But the sight of a woman's tears gets me every time. I just didn't have the heart to say no."

"Sydney...tears?" A look of sheer bewilderment shadowed Duffy's face. Sydney's face, on the other hand, had a look of sheer fury. Reese half-expected lightning bolts to shoot out of her eyes at him.

Let her put *this* in her report to Lucian, he thought smugly.

"And then I got to thinking," he went on smoothly. "And I decided that it was actually in my best interest to give Sydney my guidance. After all, it made sense to me that the wider the range of dining choices, the more customers that will be drawn to Bloomfield from neighboring towns and cities, including Philadelphia. So it also made sense that a little hands-on experience in the real world would improve Sydney's chance at success and in the long run, help us both."

"Actually, Grandfather," Sydney said through clenched teeth, "Reese is exaggerat—"

"Excellent thinking." Duffy nodded with approval. "Improved commerce in this town benefits everyone. Have you considered running for city council? This town could use a man with forward thinking like yours."

"I leave politics to experienced men such as yourself, sir." Reese knew he was laying it on a little thick, but the judge didn't seem to mind. Sydney, however, quite obviously minded a great deal. Her cheeks were flushed—this time not from kissing, but from anger—and he could swear he saw a twitch at the corner of her eye.

When Judge Howland's cell phone began to ring, he pulled it out of his pocket. While he spoke on the phone, Sydney turned her back to her grandfather and glared at Reese, silently mouthing a series of names that were extremely unladylike. Folding his arms, he leaned against the doorjamb again and smiled back at her.

When her grandfather finished his call, she snapped her mouth shut, spun around again and smiled at him.

Grumbling, the judge dropped his phone back into his pocket.

"Is something wrong, Grandfather?"

"I'm gone less than an hour and my office is already in chaos," Duffy said irritably. "The copy machine repair man blew a fuse and there's no power, and the dedication ceremony for Senator Johnson at city hall this afternoon has been moved to tomorrow morning."

Peanuts and Sydney forgotten, Duffy turned sharply on his heels. Reese could hear the judge muttering to himself until the tavern door clicked shut behind him.

Sydney stared after her grandfather, then very slowly turned back to Reese. "Tears?" she said, her voice rising an octave. "I asked *you* for help and *you* didn't have the heart to turn *me* down?"

She moved closer and jabbed one long, slender finger at his chest. "The only part of *that* you got right was the part about not having a heart. How dare you tell my grandfather that I cried to get you to help me!"

With her flushed cheeks and the blue sparks flying from her eyes, Reese thought that Sydney looked magnificent. He glanced down at her finger still poking into his chest, thought about kissing her again, but—thank Heavens—good sense prevailed.

"I saved your behind, Syd," he said evenly. "What would your grandfather say if he knew the truth, that you'd played poker with a lowly tavern owner, lost, and were paying off a bet? You should be thanking me."

"*Thanking* you?" She rolled her eyes and groaned. "After the two-hour lecture I'm going to get from my grandfather on my lack of professionalism in a business situation, then the one-hour lesson on the proper behavior for a young lady alone with a man, I'll tell you what you can do with any thanks you think you deserve.

You're the only one benefiting from this absurd bet we made, Sinclair, so don't go looking for any thanks from me.''

"Any time you want out, Syd…''

She pulled back when he reached toward her face. He plucked a peanut shell from her hair, and she frowned at him. "I finish what I start,'' she said firmly.

He grinned at her. "I'm glad to hear that, Sydney. Very glad.''

The sudden flush of pink on her high cheeks pleased Reese immensely. He leaned close, brought his mouth within a few inches of hers. Her eyelids lowered; she started to sway toward him. Then she blinked and jerked her head away.

"Oh, no.'' Peanuts crunched under her feet as she stepped back. "*That's* one thing we won't be finishing,'' she insisted. "Not gonna happen, Sinclair.''

She turned and quickly left.

He watched her go, heard the tavern door close behind her. He stood there for a long moment, staring after her.

"Don't bet on it, Syd,'' he said softly. "Just don't bet on it.''

The beveled glass and oak doors welcomed customers to Le Petit Bistro—or at least it would welcome them when the restaurant had its grand opening in a little over three weeks. The dining area was small, room enough for only ten booths and seven tables, but that suited Sydney just fine. She preferred cozy and intimate, soft music, simple elegance. Her staff was small: a college student named Becky who went to school in the mornings would be her hostess; Nell, a single mother new to Bloomfield County who had been the first applicant to respond to the waitressing ad and had been so perfect that Sydney had hired her on the spot; and Latona, an assistant chef newly graduated from a cooking school in Philadelphia. Sydney had already developed and tested her menu, ordered her supplies in advance and placed her advertisements in all the local papers. Except for the granite countertop that Lucian would be installing for her next week, everything was in place and ready to go.

Excitement rippled through her.

Hands locked behind her back, she stood in the middle of the room and smiled. The tables were bare now, but come opening night, there would be fresh flowers on pink linen tablecloths, crystal votive holders, sparkling wine goblets. She could already hear the soft murmur of conversation, the faint clink of forks and knives on china. Smell the scent of fresh herbs and vegetables and melting butter.

From the time she'd been old enough to reach the kitchen counter, she'd wanted to learn how to cook, but her mother had never allowed it. The preparation of food was for the servants, her mother had always told her. As the granddaughter of Bloomfield County's Honorable Judge Howland, Sydney was expected to receive and entertain guests with conversation of current events or charming anecdotes of family history.

Occasionally, though, Sydney would sneak into the kitchen and watch Emily, the family cook, stirring a soup on the stove or chopping celery on the heavy butcher block island. Sydney could have watched, fascinated, for hours. But her mother would always find her and drag her back to the party, reprimanding her sternly on the proper etiquette and behavior for a Howland-Taylor.

Sydney's mother had been a first-class, stiff-necked, pretentious snob.

Sydney knew that everyone in Bloomfield County thought she was just as pretentious as her mother had been. And even though it hurt, she understood why they thought that. She'd spent a lifetime behaving the way her mother had expected of her.

But Sydney knew that she was worse than a snob. Much worse.

She was a coward.

Since she was a little girl, she'd always been frightened. Afraid she might receive a grade less than an A on a test, that she might get her dress dirty or say the wrong thing. That her parents would fight if she wasn't perfect. So she always did the extra credit, was always on time, always put her clothes neatly away and never made messes.

But it hadn't mattered that she'd done all those things. Her father had still left when she was twelve and never once come back. A day had never passed that her mother didn't spew anger and malice toward him.

Never a day, to this very day, that Sydney didn't wonder if maybe, just maybe, if she hadn't made so much noise, if she'd sat up straighter or never complained about eating brussels sprouts, her father would never have left.

And then, fourteen years later, maybe Bobby wouldn't have left, either.

She knew in her heart, of course, that marriage to Bobby would never have worked, but somehow that knowledge didn't quite cushion the embarrassment of standing in the church in her wedding dress, having Theresa, her maid-of-honor, come tell her that Bobby wasn't coming. Then having to tell all the guests that the groom had taken ill and the ceremony was called off.

He was sick, all right. Sick of her.

But then, slowly, over the next few weeks, her embarrassment turned to anger, her anger to determination. Determination to courage. The courage to do what she'd always secretly wanted. Her grandfather had argued that a restaurant was a foolhardy enterprise, most failed within the first year, the work was hard, the hours long. Nothing had changed her mind.

Let everyone feel sorry for her, or think she was a snob. Le Petit Bistro would be the best darn restaurant that Bloomfield County would ever see.

And that included Squire's Tavern and Inn.

She smiled at the image of Reese opening his office door three days ago to a sea of peanuts; the stunned look on his face. He'd been so smug when he'd come back from all his errands and found her at the counter, working so submissively at shelling all those nuts. So pompous.

Her smile widened. He certainly hadn't been so smug when he'd gone down in a deluge of peanuts.

Then he'd had to go and ruin it all by kissing her.

Nobody had ever kissed her like that. Not Bobby, certainly not Ken, the manager at Bloomfield County Trust and Loan she'd dated for a short time. Not even Jean-Paul, the French pastry chef she'd gone out with several times when she'd been in Paris. They'd all paled in comparison to Reese.

She'd never forgive him for that.

Before that kiss, it had been so easy to tell herself that she would never, in a hundred years, ever fall for a man like Reese. They were so completely opposite: He was a confirmed bachelor; she wanted to settle down. He never took anything seriously; she considered herself earnest and thoughtful. And she *liked* tablecloths and flowers, which he obviously didn't.

But in spite of all that, what really frightened her was the possibility—as remote as it was—of falling in love with him and knowing that he would never love her back. At a very basic level, she was afraid he had the power to break her heart. Not just a crack, like with Bobby, but complete annihilation. She'd moved on with her life, she had her restaurant. She wasn't willing to risk it with him.

And still, every time she thought of that kiss, every time she remembered the way his fingers had skimmed her leg, the way his palm had cupped her breast, her skin felt tight and hot, her pulse quickened and she had to remind herself to breathe.

Damn you, Sinclair!

Well, she'd just have to deal with it, she decided and snatched up a rag she'd been using to dust. She acknowledged her attraction, but she'd managed to keep her distance from him the past three days while she'd been working for him in the evenings. She could continue to do just that. And he'd kept his distance from her, too. He'd probably put the kiss out of his mind completely, she thought, pouring a little lemon beeswax onto the rag and rubbing furiously at the buffet table she'd placed in the entryway of the café. No doubt that sort of thing happened to Reese Sinclair all the time. One more woman, one more kiss in a long line of swooning females, she suspected. As long as she kept her feet on the ground and was sensible, she'd be safe.

"Sandpaper usually works better if you're trying to remove the stain."

With a squeak, she spun around at the sound of

Reese's deep voice behind her. Heavens! It was bad enough he infiltrated her mind, did he have to turn up in the flesh, as well?

"Reese!" Her voice was much too high-pitched and breathless. She cleared her throat. "You startled me."

"Sorry." Smiling, he nodded at the rag in her hand. "I wasn't sure if you were punishing that wood or polishing it."

She wasn't sure, either, since she'd been thinking about Reese. Afraid that he'd see it in her eyes, she kept her attention on the buffet and continued her buffing. "What brings you by?"

Why did he have to stand so close? she thought irritably. And why did he have to look so incredibly handsome wearing faded blue jeans and a moss green T-shirt that made his eyes look like a dark, mysterious forest?

Damn him.

"I brought you flowers."

Her heart skipped. He'd brought her flowers? Maybe he'd said flour, like for baking. Though that wouldn't make sense, either. She glanced up cautiously. "You what?"

"Flowers. I brought you flowers."

No man had ever bought her flowers. She felt a hitch in her chest. "You did?"

"Yeah." He gestured toward the open front door. "I don't know what they're called. The nursery guy said you could plant them now and they shouldn't die, at least not until we get a heavy snow."

She looked out the door and saw several colorful pots sitting next to the raised brick bed that Boomer was so fond of digging in.

He hadn't brought her flowers.

Well, he'd brought her flowers, she corrected, but he hadn't brought her *flowers*.

Of course he hadn't brought her flowers.

And the fact that she'd thought—for just an instant—that he had made her feel like a complete fool. An idiot.

"Thank you." She turned her attention back to her polishing. If she looked at him, she was afraid he'd see in her eyes what she'd been thinking and then he'd know what a little fool she was.

"My gardener from the tavern will be over later to plant them," he said. "I'd do it, but I'd probably cause more damage than Boomer trying to dig them up."

"Thank you, but I'd rather do it myself." She knelt in front of the buffet and began to polish the legs.

"It's my responsibility, Syd."

"I prefer to do it myself."

"Sydney. I think we should…well, we should talk."

He hunkered down beside her, stilled her hand with his. She cursed the thump of her heart. Cursed him. She knew she should stand, that she shouldn't let him this close, but she stayed where she was, her knees nearly touching his. "All right."

"I don't want you to come to the tavern anymore."

She doubted a physical slap would have hurt as much as the verbal hit he'd just given her. The cold gripping her chest made it hard to breathe. She tugged her hand out from under his and forced her attention back to the legs of the buffet. "All right."

He ran a hand through his thick hair and sighed. "God, that's not what I meant. I meant I don't want you *working* at the tavern anymore."

Oh, gosh, that made her feel *so* much better. Careful to keep herself composed, she continued polishing the wood, kept her strokes smooth and controlled. She *refused* to let him see her cry. "All right."

He took hold of her arms and turned her toward him. "Stop saying all right. It's not all right. And I'm not saying what I mean."

"Then why don't you?" she said coolly.

"Sydney, this isn't…I didn't…" He sighed. "Dammit, Syd, what I'm trying to say is I'm sorry. You had every right to be angry about Boomer digging up your flowers. I never should have made that bet with you."

"Then why did you?" She forced herself to concentrate on his surprise apology, refused to think about the feel of his strong hands on her arms and what had happened the last time he'd gotten this close and touched her. She knew if she did that every vow she'd made to keep her distance would fly out the window and she'd tackle him right here and now, and make him kiss her again. Touch her again.

And more.

"I don't know," he said, interrupting her wayward thoughts. "Maybe it was the way you flew into the tavern with Boomer in your arms. Your hair looking like you'd just climbed out of bed and your eyes flashing blue fire. The way you looked down at me with that arrogant little nose of yours, issuing ultimatums. I had to do something."

In spite of the heat rippling across her skin, she arched one eyebrow. "Oh?"

"See?" He smiled. "There it goes again. If I can admit I'm a jerk, you can at least admit you're a snob."

She sniffed. "I'm not a snob."

Now he raised a brow and looked at her doubtfully.

"Well, maybe it seems that way," she relented. "But I'm just…conscientious."

His brow went up higher.

She pursed her lips. "Oh, all right. Maybe sometimes I do set my expectations a little high. Maybe sometimes I am a snob. There. Are you happy?"

"It's a start." He smiled at her, loosened his hold on her arms and slid his hands up to her shoulders. "I just wanted to see you loosen up a little."

"Maybe I don't want to loosen up." Especially right now. If she loosened up now, the way he was touching her shoulders, she'd slide her arms around his neck and press her lips to his. "Maybe I like being just the way I am. And you like being the way you are."

"Oh?" He cocked his head. "And what way am I?"

Sexy as hell. Handsome. Rugged. Strong. She started to lean toward him....

*Stop that.*

"Frivolous."

He chuckled, slid his thumbs back and forth over her collarbone. "I'm not frivolous, Syd. I'm spontaneous. You should try it sometime."

It took every ounce of willpower to focus on his words, not on the way his thumbs were moving sensuously over her skin, or the warmth spreading like molten lava through her limbs. "You've obviously forgotten about Monday," she insisted. "If that wasn't spontaneous, then I don't know what is."

"I haven't forgotten anything. In fact, Sydney," he said with a slow smile, "I remember everything. In detail."

When his dark green gaze dropped to her mouth, her breath caught in her throat. "It—that—was a mistake, Reese. I was...we just—"

"Went a little nuts?"

She couldn't stop the smile on her lips any more than

the furious pounding of her heart. "Something like that. It was nice and all that, but I want you to know I realize it was just one of those caught-up-in-the-moment-things. You don't have to worry about it."

"You know, Syd," he said with a touch of exasperation, "I just might believe that if I hadn't been there. It was a hell of a lot more than nice, sweetheart. You were as hot for me as I was for you. If your grandfather hadn't walked in when he had, you would have been in my bed, begging me for more."

Her cheeks burned at the accuracy of his evaluation. She would have begged, dammit. Still, she started to protest until he slid his hands up the side of her neck and pulled her closer. "Go ahead and deny it," he said tightly. "Just say it one more time."

She snapped her mouth shut. It was a dare and she knew it. They both knew if he kissed her again what would happen. Where it would go.

And she couldn't go there with Reese. She didn't have the courage. She pulled away from him and stood, twisted the rag in her hand to keep from reaching for him.

"All right," she said, hating the little quiver in her voice. "I admit it. It was more than nice. But it's *not* going to happen again. A quick roll in the hay might be right up your alley, but sex is something special to me. It's more than an itch and more than a 'spontaneous' tumble into bed with the closest warm body."

He stood slowly, and the desire she'd seen in his eyes only moments before now turned to anger. She hadn't meant to, but she'd gone too far. She should apologize, she knew she should, but it was easier this way. This way, he'd walk away and stay away.

"You think whatever you like, Syd," he said tightly.

"But if you really believe all that bull, then you're going to spend a lot of lonely nights in a very cold bed."

She felt the tears gather in the back of her throat as he turned and walked toward the door.

"Reese?"

He stopped, but didn't turn around.

"There's no reason we can't be friends," she said carefully. "If you need help at the tavern, I don't mind."

"Thanks, Syd, but it won't be necessary. I'll manage just fine." He started to walk away again, but she called his name one more time. He waited.

"Thank you," she said. "For the flowers."

He nodded stiffly, then glanced over his shoulder at her. "I almost forgot. My sister wants you to call her. Something about a last-minute catering job for Gabe and Melanie's surprise engagement party tomorrow night."

He left before she could reply, and she stared at the empty doorway long after he was gone.

# Seven

Sinclair family events were always noisy and the surprise party on Saturday night was no exception. Everyone was already waiting in the small private dining room at the back of the tavern when Gabe and Melanie showed up for what they thought was a typical get-together of "pizza and beer." They were not expecting an elegant celebration that included candles and white roses and a lavish five course French meal, prepared and served by Sydney Taylor.

Because the tavern was open for business, Reese split his time between the party and handling the busy Saturday night crowd. He'd rearranged schedules so he'd have a full crew, but at the moment he was filling in for Jimmy, his bartender, while he took a break. So far tonight there'd been no crises or problems that had demanded his attention.

Unless he considered Sydney in one of those categories.

Crises. No.

Problem. Yes.

He'd been angry when he'd left her place two days ago. Furious, even, with her assumption that he'd simply wanted a "quick roll in the hay" as she'd so delicately put it.

Not that he really knew *what* he'd wanted from her, or where their unexpected attraction would end up. He just didn't like her assessment of his morals, or lack of them. So maybe he had dated a lot of women. That didn't mean he didn't have scruples. And it certainly didn't mean he simply had an "itch," and she'd been the "closest warm body."

He clenched his jaw just thinking about her.

Lord, the woman made him crazy.

While he filled a pitcher of beer for Judy, one of his waitresses, he watched as Sydney came out of the kitchen carrying a tray loaded with steaming bread puddings. Since her kitchen wouldn't be fully operable until her oven was calibrated, she'd needed to use his to prepare the meal for this evening. When she'd come over yesterday during lunch to ask him if it would be all right, he'd said sure, then quickly turned his attention back to filling drinks for the thirsty noon crowd.

But even after he'd turned away from her, he'd been aware of her standing there, her shoulders stiff and chin lifted, looking as if she still had something to say.

Well, they'd said enough, he'd thought. More than enough. He wasn't about to waste his time thinking about Sydney Taylor night and day.

Thinking about how soft her skin was, wondering what it would feel like when he untied that knot of pretty hair at the top of her head and dragged his fingers through the loosened strands, what she would do when he slipped his hands under that pink silk blouse she had on tonight....

"Uh, I think that's probably full enough," Reese heard a woman say hesitantly.

"What?" Reese snapped his mind back to the present and looked at Judy, realized she'd been talking to him. She nodded toward the pitcher he was filling. Beer flowed over the sides.

"Damn," he muttered, releasing the valve and reaching for a towel. Damn, damn, *damn.*

Shaking her head, Judy poured off the excess, grabbed four cold mugs, then headed off to a table of construction workers that were currently on Sinclair Construction's payroll.

He glanced over as Sydney passed. He couldn't help but appreciate the sway of her slender hips under the crisp, white chef's apron she wore. Underneath the apron a pretty floral skirt skimmed those long legs of hers. He glanced back up at her face, noticed the flush of pleasure on her cheeks and the brightness in her eyes.

His throat turned to dust.

She'd looked like that right after he'd kissed her the other day, he remembered, only this time her pleasure was due to her excitement over Cara hiring her to prepare the food for the party. He hadn't seen what the big deal was all about, or even why Cara had hired Sydney at all. They could have celebrated just as well with pizza or hamburgers or Corky's famous chili. What was the point of all that fancy French cooking?

And then he'd tasted her ravioli stuffed with lobster and shrimp, drenched in a sauce. He'd actually moaned, it was so good. And so was the chicken and mushroom dish she'd made for a main course. That had been a taste of heaven, too.

So she could cook, he thought begrudgingly. Maybe she wasn't just some bored rich girl who thought owning a restaurant would be fun. He'd seen how hard she worked, and when Sydney set her mind to something, she was stubborn as a bulldog about it.

Too damn stubborn.

Well, he didn't need stubborn. And he sure as hell didn't need Sydney Taylor messing up his mind and his life. He'd been perfectly content before he'd locked horns with her, and he intended to go right back. She wasn't coming to the tavern to work anymore, and though he'd actually missed her the past two days, he didn't miss the aggravation. His life was back to simple and quiet, and he liked it exactly that way.

After tonight, he wouldn't give Sydney another thought.

Except for maybe every time he laid eyes on a peanut.

"Hey, Reese." A mug of beer already in her hand, Rhonda Waters sidled onto the bar stool across from him. "Where you been keeping yourself?"

"Right here waiting for you, honey," he bantered with the attractive brunette.

"You two-timing me, sugar?" Mary Lou Simpson, her new hair dye as red as a tomato, slid onto the bar stool next to Rhonda. "Shame on you. And here I voted for you in the Bloomfield County Best Butt contest. You could at least show a little appreciation."

Reese had always thought the whole business of that award had been good for a laugh. Suddenly it didn't seem so funny anymore. If anything, it was starting to annoy him.

He forced a smile, wished that Jimmy would hurry and get back from his break.

"So, Reese." Mary Lou leaned against the bar counter in an obvious attempt to reveal her ample bosom. "When we gonna go out driving? I've got a brand new convertible Camaro, and it's not too cold out yet to put the top down."

His smile still frozen in place, Reese cocked his head and raised a brow at Mary Lou's blatant innuendo. "Well, now, Mary Lou, soon as I have a full staff, maybe we'll talk about that." *Or maybe we won't...* Definitely won't, he decided.

Rhonda choked on her beer, then giggled. Mary Lou's eyes widened, then she purred, "I can hardly wait, sugar."

Oh, dammit! Reese groaned silently. That wasn't what he'd meant to say. He'd meant to say crew, not *staff*.

He glanced around the room, searching for any sign of Jimmy, then grabbed a towel and started wiping up an imaginary spill.

"I heard you been hanging around Sydney Taylor," Rhonda said, sipping on her beer. "You got something going with her?"

"Don't be ridiculous," Mary Lou said with a laugh. "What would Reese possibly see in someone like Sydney the Hun? What would *any* man see in her, for that matter?"

"True." Rhonda nodded. "Even Bobby got smart before he made the mistake of tying himself down to Sour Face Sydney."

"Hey, now," Reese said tightly, struggling to contain his anger, "just wait a—"

He stopped midsentence.

Sydney stood directly behind the two women. He'd been so distracted with Rhonda and Mary Lou's annoying insults regarding Sydney, he hadn't noticed her come up.

Maybe she hadn't heard.

"Hello, Rhonda. Mary Lou."

Oh, hell. Reese groaned inwardly. Based on the icicles dripping from her hello, she'd heard, all right.

Eyes wide, backs stiff, Rhonda and Mary Lou slowly turned and squeaked back a hello. *Ha,* Reese thought. *Serves you both right for being so nasty.*

"Sorry to hear about your job, Mary Lou," Sydney said, her cool gaze locked on the redhead. "I'm sure you'll find another employer who will appreciate your *qualifications* as much as John Sweeney did."

Everyone in town knew that Mary Lou had been sleeping with the owner of Sweeney's Sporting Goods. Well, everyone except Mrs. Sweeney, of course. Until she'd caught the two of them after hours, in the store's bass boat, wearing nothing but waders and surprised expressions. There were instant employment changes, which included an in-store, full-time position for Colleen Sweeney where she could keep a close eye on her philandering husband, and the boot for Mary Lou.

Sydney turned her attention to Rhonda. "And I'm sorry about Mike and you, too."

Rhonda narrowed her eyes. "Sorry about what?"

"That you broke up after such a long time," Sydney said, the sympathy heavy in her voice. "It must be hard for you."

"He's got a carpentry job in Ridgeway, that's all," Rhonda insisted. "That's why he's been gone so much. Even tonight he's working overtime on a job there and—" She stopped suddenly, doubt darkening her brown eyes. "Ah, well, I gotta run, Syd. Nice to see you."

Rhonda slid off the chair and headed for the pay phone by the restrooms. Mary Lou followed.

Reese stared at Sydney, a mixture of admiration and awe at the way she'd handled the two women.

"Your family would like you to come in and say goodbye when you have a minute," she said evenly.

"Thanks." He wasn't sure what else to say. She should be angry, he thought. Mad as hell. He knew *he* was. But Sydney stood there as calm as could be. As if nothing at all had just happened. As if it didn't matter to her in the slightest that these two women had insulted her.

"Thank you for letting me use the tavern's kitchen tonight, Reese," she said with a politeness that irritated him. "I'll just gather up my things from the back dining room and be out of your way."

"Okay." *But it's not okay. Dammit, Sydney, can't you just let yourself go and be mad? Yell or scream or hit something?* He sure as hell would. But not Sydney, he thought. Not cool, calm, collected Sydney. Nothing got through that thick skin of hers. And no one.

He watched her turn smoothly and head back through the thinning crowd in the tavern, then disappear down the hallway that led to the back dining room and his office.

Well, fine then, dammit. He wasn't about to waste his time worrying about Sydney. She could take care of herself. She didn't need him; she'd made that perfectly clear. As far as he was concerned, Sydney was ancient history.

Sydney felt Reese's gaze on her as she walked away from the bar, knew that he'd expected some kind of reaction from her after hearing Mary Lou and Rhonda's cruel comments. But Sydney had learned long ago to hide her feelings, to pretend everything was all right when it really wasn't. She'd learned to tuck every emotion into a tiny little spot inside of her, then wait until she was completely alone and no one would see the truth. That was the only time she'd let herself really feel.

She focused on her legs instead of the pain gripping her chest, ordered her knees not to buckle, to hold firm and carry her out of the tavern, down the hallway, past the dining room, past Reese's office, then to the back door that led to the outside garden.

Quietly she closed the door behind her, thankful that the night air was crisp and the garden dark, lit only from the soft light of a half-moon. She shivered, made it down two steps before her legs refused to listen to her anymore. She sank down on the steps, dropped her head into her shaking hands and let the tears come.

Sydney the Hun.

Sour Face Sydney.

She'd always known what people thought of her, that they didn't like her, but to actually hear those terrible things spoken aloud only confirmed what she'd always believed.

No one could ever love her. Not her father, not her mother. Not Bobby.

Certainly not Reese.

Mary Lou and Rhonda's words might have been cruel, but they were true. And the realization of that, the conscious acceptance of it as the truth, was like a dam breaking inside her. A tidal wave of hurt and pain rolled through her, and this time she was helpless to stop it. So she let it go.

In long, choking sobs and hot, endless tears, she simply let it go.

She felt the nudge on her arm, the cold, wet nose, and realized that Boomer had joined her on the step. He whimpered, then licked her face. Sydney slipped an arm around the dog, dragged her fingers through his thick fur and actually laughed at the irony of Boomer being the only one who seemed to really like her.

It had been such a wonderful evening. Preparing the meal, serving each course, seeing the pleasure on everyone's face when they tried each dish. She'd even heard Reese moan when he'd tried the lobster-and-shrimp ravioli.

And then she'd chosen exactly the wrong time to walk up and hear things about herself she'd never wanted to hear.

A fresh round of tears burst forth and she hugged the dog tightly to her.

"Sydney."

She heard her name called softly, then the touch of a hand on her shoulder.

*Not Reese,* she thought miserably. *Anyone but Reese.*

"Go away."

He didn't. Instead he sat down beside her and put his arm around her. He touched her wet cheek. "You're crying."

Humiliated, she turned her head from him. "No, I'm not. I never cry. Crying is for pathetic, helpless females," she managed to sob out through a fresh round of tears.

He chuckled, then pulled her closer. "Sydney, you are as far from pathetic and helpless as a person can get."

She shook her head to disagree, then laid her cheek on the shoulder he offered. When her tears eased and the shuddering finally ceased, she drew in a deep breath then let it out again.

"Better?" he asked quietly.

With a sniff, she nodded, then tried to sit up.

"Just be still for a minute," he said and drew her back into his arms.

*Just for a minute,* she told herself and let herself relax against his strong, warm body.

The sound of gurgling water from the fountain filled the cool evening air, and the scent of the last roses of the season drifted from the overhead arbor. In spite of her embarrassment, she couldn't remember when she'd felt such peace or tranquility.

They were quiet for several minutes, just listening to the sounds of the night and Boomer's soft panting.

"There were one hundred and fifty people in the church," she said, breaking the silence. "My maid-of-honor had just put my wedding veil on me and we were looking in the mirror, smiling at each other when the wedding director came in. I knew something was wrong. I thought maybe Bobby was sick or he'd had a terrible accident." She laughed dryly. "He had an accident, all right. With your cocktail waitress. The note he'd sent just said that he was sorry."

Reese swore under his breath. "I never could stand that guy. He was a jerk."

"I thought my life was over. I thought maybe I'd just move rather than face everyone again, knowing they were whispering behind my back." She closed her eyes, felt a single tear slide from the corner of her eye. "It hurt, Reese," she whispered.

"I know, baby."

"Almost as much as when my father left and never came back. Almost as much as when people call me Sydney the Hun or Sour Face Sydney."

She shivered when he brushed her cheek with his thumb and wiped away the tear. "Mary Lou and Rhonda are shallow, empty-headed bimbos. They couldn't hold a candle to you."

"You're just saying that."

"I'm saying it because it's true, sweetheart. You've got something no one can buy or fake. You've got spirit and integrity and an intensity about you that energizes the entire room whenever you walk in."

She blinked, then swallowed the lump in her throat. Had he really called her baby and sweetheart? And had he really said all those nice things about her?

And more important, had he meant them?

The moon shed enough light onto his face that she could see he *was* telling the truth. That he meant every word.

And through the pain she felt joy, a weight lifting off her chest and a swelling in her heart.

"I think you're wonderful with people." She straightened, looked into his eyes. "You know how to make people relax and have a good time. Laugh. I could never do that."

"Sure you could." He tucked a wayward strand of her hair behind her ear. "You just need to loosen up a little, Syd. Not take everything so seriously all the time. Let yourself go once in a while."

Everything in her entire life had been carefully planned, every sock neatly folded and put in the correct drawer, every slip of paper properly filed. Each "bunny in its own basket," as her mother used to say.

Could she let go?

She desperately wanted to do just that. To let herself go. Not think about anything but the moment and what felt good. Like the touch of Reese's fingertips on her ear, or the feel of his strong arm around her waist.

But she wanted more. Much more.

She didn't know how to tell Reese what she wanted, but she let instinct guide her. She touched his cheek with her hand; the strength she felt there gave her the confidence she so lacked.

"You were right, you know," she whispered.

He covered her hand with his, brought it to his mouth and gently kissed her fingers. "About what?"

His firm lips against her made her insides curl, gave her the courage to continue. "What you said about my grandfather interrupting us," she murmured. "If he hadn't, I would have been in your bed, begging you to make love to me."

Reese went very still. She felt a moment of panic that he wasn't feeling what she was feeling, that he didn't want her. If he pushed her away, she couldn't bear it.

But then she saw his gaze darken and narrow and the look of intensity in his eyes made her heart skip. She felt his jaw tighten under the palm of her hand. She leaned her body toward him, brought her lips close to his.

"Sydney, this might not be a good time—"

So she had been wrong. Pain ripped through her chest and she pulled her hand away and forced a smile. "Of course not. You're right. I—I don't know what I was thinking. I'm sorry."

"Dammit, Sydney." His voice was a soft growl as he took hold of her shoulders and forced her to face him. "Don't look at me like that. You're upset right now, you might not be thinking clearly."

She dared to put her hand on his chest, felt the rapid beat of his heart. It matched her own. "I'm thinking more clearly than I have in years." She kept her gaze level with his. "I know what I want. Do you?"

His hands tightened on her arms, and she felt a shudder move through him.

He nodded slowly, narrowed his eyes. "I want you, Sydney." His arms came around her, dragged her tightly against him. "I want you."

He crushed his mouth to hers, a demanding, forceful kiss that took her breath away. *I want you.* Sydney had waited to hear those words her entire life. She knew this was just about sex, not love, but still it didn't matter. For this moment, she was the happiest woman in the world.

His kiss thrilled her, made her mind spin and her pulse race. A lifetime of yearning spilled through her, yearning and desire, as hot as it was impatient.

She felt his impatience as well, his desire, as he deepened the kiss, slanting his mouth over hers again and again. She answered him, shivering with excitement, with anticipation.

His mouth still on hers, he scooped her up in his arms and stood. She wound her arms around his neck and clung to him, never wanting the kiss to end. The scent of his skin, as rugged as it was masculine, filled her senses. She felt safe and protected in his strong, steady arms.

As if she'd come home.

Not the home she'd been raised in. That had never been a home. But really home, a place where she belonged.

The realization frightened her, and the implications that came with it nearly had her pulling away. But she'd been a coward for far too long. She would not let this moment slip by her, would not let her fear deny herself this pleasure.

Just this once, she would let herself feel, just feel. No logic, no reason, no arguments. Just sheer, unfettered bliss.

Smiling softly, she laid her head on his broad shoulder.

Reese carried Sydney—not back into the tavern, which would be the wisest course of action—but to the front door of his cottage. Even if he'd wanted to take her back into the tavern, which he didn't, he didn't want anyone else to see her tearstained cheeks or red eyes. He felt strangely possessive of her at the moment, still angry at Rhonda and Mary Lou for their asinine remarks.

But he was the biggest idiot of all for not realizing how deeply the two women had hurt Sydney. He'd simply assumed—and that was certainly the appropriate word—that no one could hurt Sydney. That she was too tough.

Only she wasn't so tough, after all. What she showed on the surface wasn't what she really was at all. Underneath all that pluck and sass, she was soft and tender. Under that cool composure she was warm and vulnerable.

He'd known something was wrong when Gabe told him that she hadn't come back into the dining room to say goodbye. After his family had left, he looked in his office and she hadn't been there, either. And since she'd gone down the hall and hadn't come back, that had only left outside.

The sight of her tears, the sound of her small sobs, had ripped through his gut like a sharp knife. He'd watched her hug Boomer tightly to her and he'd never felt so damn helpless in his life.

He tightened his hold on her, reluctant to set her down as he stepped onto his porch. He fumbled awkwardly with the knob and Sydney reached down, pushed his hand away, then opened the door.

His living room was dark, but the soft glow from a bedside lamp shone through the half-open door of his bedroom.

"Sydney," he said hoarsely. "Are you sure?"

She smiled softly, pressed her lips to his.

Stunned by the force of the need pulsating through his blood, he carried her to his bed.

# Eight

Sydney had never known that spontaneity could feel so wonderful. So liberating.

So exhilarating.

Reese crossed the distance to his big, beautiful four poster bed and it was all Sydney could do not to jump out of his arms onto the mattress and drag him down with her. She felt giddy with excitement and anticipation.

He lowered her not onto the bed, but let her slide slowly, sensuously down him until the tips of her feet touched the floor. She felt the tug on her apron strings behind her back, then the slide of the garment off her shoulders and down her body until it fell at her feet. Afraid that her knees wouldn't hold her, she kept her arms wound tightly around his neck. When she lifted her face to his, she saw the desire burning in his dark gaze, the need, and she shuddered from the force of it.

Yet he held back, waiting.

She smiled at him, brought her lips an inch from his. "You're going to make me beg, aren't you, Sinclair?" She brushed her lips lightly against his, whispered, "Make love to me, Reese. Please make love to me."

Her feet came off the floor as he dragged her upwards again, cupping her bottom as he lifted her, fitting her intimately against him. If there had been any doubt of his need before, there was certainly none now. His mouth all but consumed her in a hungry rush of frantic kisses.

And then, as if in slow motion, they were moving backward. As one, they glided down to the bed. Sydney sank into the soft mattress, easily took the weight of Reese's strong body on top of hers, thought it was the most glorious feeling in the world.

Until his open mouth moved down her neck. Oh, *that* was glorious, too. She felt the buttons of her blouse open one by one, then the slide of silk over her skin. He flipped open the snap at the front of her white lace bra, but instead of his hand, he used his teeth to tug the soft fabric aside. She felt the rush of cool air on her bare breasts, then the rush of his warm breath.

Gasping, she arched upward.

His mouth was hot on her soft flesh, his hands were gentle and kneading. And when he pulled the sensitive tip of one breast into his mouth and laved the nipple with his hot tongue, she moaned.

She'd been wrong. *This* was the most glorious feeling in the world. Intense pleasure rippled in hot waves through her, pooling between her legs. On a whimper, she raked her fingers through his thick, dark hair and moved against him.

He took his time, his hands and mouth giving equal

attention to each breast, until she felt like soft taffy, her insides pulling and stretching, over and over.

"Reese," she gasped, her hands moving restlessly over his back, his shoulders. "Please…"

He rose over her then and the soft light of the bedroom lamp shone in his dark, passion-glazed eyes. His face was hard and angular, his jaw tight, his hair rumpled as he stared down at her.

"You are so beautiful," he said hoarsely.

"Thank you," she said breathlessly, realized dimly that even in the heat of passion, a lifetime of impeccable manners could not be ignored. She also supposed that this was the proper pillow talk she'd only heard of, but never experienced. *You're beautiful, the only one. I love you….* The things that people were supposed to say when they made love, even though they didn't mean them.

He shook his head slowly and sighed. "You don't believe me, do you? I can see it in your eyes that you don't. I want you to look at me, Syd. Look in my eyes."

Through the haze of desire humming through her body, she did as he asked.

"You're beautiful," he repeated softly. "You might make me crazy sometimes and confuse the hell out of me, but you're the most beautiful woman I've ever seen."

He *did* mean it, she realized. Her heart soared, and she had to quickly blink back the moisture in her eyes before she ruined the moment with silly tears. His words gave her courage, unleashed the last thread of inhibition inside her.

She rose up, slid her hands over his chest and rolled on top of him as she eased him onto his back. The surprise in his eyes delighted her almost as much as the

sudden feeling of power she gained from this new position.

Her gaze held his as she slowly drew her blouse off
her shoulders, then her bra, and tossed them onto the
floor beside the bed. His eyes grew dark and intense as
he watched her.

"Those clothes might get wrinkled," he teased. "Are
you sure you don't want to fold them?"

"Nope." Smiling softly, she reached behind her
head.

Reese's breath caught in his throat as he watched
Sydney stretch her long, lovely arms up and behind her
head in a seductive pose that made his blood boil. One
at a time, she pulled the pins from the knot of hair
coiled on top of her head and tossed them with her
clothes. When the last pin was removed, her hair tumbled down around her soft shoulders like a curtain of
gold silk. Her eyes had turned a smoky blue, her skin
was smooth as the finest porcelain. His gaze traveled
lower and his heart slammed in his chest at the beautiful
sight of her soft, full breasts and the rosy, hardened
peaks that he'd tasted only moments ago.

He wanted more.

He reached for her, but she shook her head and
pushed his hands to his sides. "You have too many
clothes on," she purred.

Her long, tapered fingers moved over his buttons until
his shirt was open, then she slipped her hands inside
and slid them over his bare chest, raking her fingernails
lightly over his skin and through the dark hair on his
chest. He sucked in a breath when she moved lower,
over his belly, tugged his shirt from his pants, then
reached for his belt buckle and pulled it open.

She glanced upward, met his gaze with hers, gave

him a slow, wicked smile that made his heart hammer furiously against his ribs. Gone was the proper Ms. Sydney Taylor: in her place was a siren. A temptress. And still there was an innocence that shimmered through those sexy eyes of hers that excited him more than any other woman had before.

Her hands moved lower; she leaned forward and blazed hot little kisses over his chest. He gritted his teeth, sucked in a sharp breath at the touch of her fingers slowly, methodically, deliberately inching down the zipper of his slacks.

When he couldn't stand it anymore, he took hold of her shoulders and flipped her onto her back, rolling with her. She gasped at the sudden movement, then just as quickly wrapped her arms around his neck. He crushed his mouth to hers while he kicked off shoes and slacks, then slid her skirt and underwear down her hips in one smooth move, taking her low-heeled black shoes with the garments and tossing everything into the pile she'd already created.

And then there was only skin touching skin.

He moved over her, kissed her temple, her cheek, the pulse at the base of her throat and an especially sensitive spot on her earlobe that made her moan. When he moved away for no more than a fraction of a moment to reach into the nightstand, she whimpered softly, called him back. Without missing a beat, he picked up where he'd left off at her earlobe and worked his way down again.

She writhed underneath him, murmured his name, whispered her pleasure while her hands moved over him, driving him as crazy as he drove her.

The heat burst into flames, consuming them. When they were both frantic with need, when he thought he would die if he waited another moment, he moved between her legs and thrust hard inside her.

Her nails dug into his back as she cried out softly.

He slammed to a stop.

"Sydney..." He struggled to speak, but it was difficult to think or form words since most of the blood from his brain had gone south. And the realization hit him like a Mack truck.

Sydney had never done this before. She was a *virgin*.

"Don't stop, Reese," she pleaded. "Please don't stop."

"But—"

"It doesn't matter." She tightened her legs around him and moved her body, confusing him, exciting him even in the midst of this unexpected revelation.

"Of course it matters," he said raggedly. "You never...you should have..."

She lifted her mouth to his and stopped his words, stopped any and all rational thoughts with her hands and her body. It was impossible not to move with the slow thrust of her hips, impossible to think of anything but the need clawing at his insides.

She set the pace and he followed, the urgency building and spiraling, coiling inside tighter and tighter.

He heard the sound of her gasp, felt the shudders ripple through her body into his, and he went over the edge with her.

She thought she would never move again. She would simply lie here forever on this big, wonderful bed, with her arms and legs twined around Reese, listening to the rapid sound of his heart beating against her own. Wanting the moment to last, she kept her eyes closed and held very still.

Her skin still tingled all over, right down to the tips of her toes. Her insides were the consistency of warm butter, and in spite of the weight of Reese's body on top of her own, she felt as if she were floating.

She now knew the *true* meaning of glorious.

"I'm too heavy for you," she heard him say. When he started to pull away, she mumbled a complaint and tightened her hold on him.

He compromised by raising himself on his elbows, then kissed her temple and cheek, then lightly brushed her lips with his. Slowly, reluctantly, she opened her eyes and looked up at him. His brow was knotted, his mouth set firm.

"Did I hurt you?"

She shook her head, smiled. "Is it always that wonderful?"

She didn't care how naive she knew she must sound. After a life-altering experience like that, what did it matter?

He smiled back at her. "No, Syd. It isn't always that wonderful."

Her smile dipped. "Does that mean it's usually better, or worse?"

Chuckling, he slid his hands up her arms. "It doesn't get better than that, Syd."

"Really? I mean, just because it was incredible for me, doesn't mean that it was—"

"Sydney. Shut up, will you?"

He covered her mouth with his before she could protest, kissed her hard and deep and endlessly.

Was it possible to want this again so soon? she wondered as his hand skimmed her waist then slipped up to caress her breast.

Obviously it was.

She let herself go, gave herself up once again to the kaleidoscope of sensations and couldn't remember once in her entire life when she'd ever been happier.

It was dark when he woke. His brain was still thick from sleep and the dream he'd had about climbing a tall, steep, snow-covered mountain, only to break through the clouds and discover a lush green meadow with wildflowers at the peak.

He scrubbed a hand over his face and thought of Sydney, then smiled. Geez, talk about symbolism.

He could hear her rustling close by, but when he reached for her she wasn't beside him. Frowning, he sat up and turned on the bedside lamp. She was dressed, on the floor beside the bed, on her hands and knees. Her head popped up when the light flooded the room.

"What are you doing?" he asked, his voice rough from sleep, or rather the lack of it. The clock on the nightstand said 3:00 a.m. They'd only gone to sleep maybe a half hour ago. At least *he* had. Apparently Sydney hadn't been asleep at all.

"I'm sorry I woke you." She had one shoe in her hand and was looking for the other.

"I asked you what you were doing?" he repeated, irritated that she was dressed and crawling around on the floor when she should be in bed with him.

"Well, it's so late and I didn't want to assume that I, well, that I should…" Her voice trailed off as she stared at the shoe in her hand.

"Spend the night?" he finished for her.

She nodded, but still wouldn't look at him.

She squeaked when he reached out unexpectedly and dragged her back into bed, then rolled her underneath him.

"Love 'em and leave 'em, huh?" He stared down at her, saw the tinge of pink on her cheeks. "Sydney Taylor, you are heartless."

"I'm sorry." Her thick lashes fluttered downward. "I just wasn't sure…I didn't know what I should do."

"Sydney." She looked so damn tempting, he thought. After making love with the woman half the night and only thirty minutes of sleep, all he had to do was look at her and he was hard again. "One of us has too many clothes on."

"I suppose that would be me." She smiled demurely.

"Looks like we have to start all over again from the beginning." He began to unbutton her blouse, then slid the soft fabric open. "This might take a few hours."

"Promise?" she asked, wrapping her arms around his neck and pulling him down to her.

He smiled against her warm, willing lips. "Promise."

Early morning light filtered in through the wooden blinds on Reese's bedroom windows. Sydney listened to the quiet, the distant sound of birdsong, and the steady, secure beating of Reese's heart.

She lay snuggled in the crook of his arm and watched him sleep. A dark shock of hair fell forward onto his forehead and she resisted the urge to slip her fingers through the errant strands and comb them back. Resisted the urge to press her cheek to his and feel the rough, short stubble of his morning beard against her smooth skin.

Resisted the urge to slide her hands over his broad, muscled chest and arms, his flat stomach and lean hips.

And more.

Smiling, she watched him instead. The slow rise and fall of his chest, the light flutter of his thick lashes, the occasional twitch of his strong jaw. He had the muscled, hard body of an athlete and though she'd experienced firsthand that strength last night, she'd also experienced his tenderness. He'd been a wonderful lover, forceful at times, yet gentle and thoughtful, too.

Lover. The word danced through her head, then rippled like warm waves over her skin. At twenty-six years old, Sydney Marie Taylor was no longer a virgin.

Her smile widened.

"When a woman smiles like that," Reese said in a sleep-roughened voice, "she's got something wicked on her mind."

Startled, Sydney felt her cheeks warm. It surprised her that after last night she would feel any embarrassment at all with Reese, but she was glad to see she still had at least some sense of propriety left.

"Certainly not," she said primly. "My thoughts are pure and chaste and—"

She gasped softly as he rolled her onto her back and covered her mouth with his. It wasn't a gentle kiss, it was possessive and insistent. Her hands slid up the warm skin on his back. When he pulled his mouth away, she kept her eyes closed and continued, though more breathlessly this time "—benevolent. The epitome of goodness and piety—"

His mouth swooped down again and she wrapped her arms around his neck, drawing him closer still. This time when he pulled away from her, his hands slid up her waist and cupped her breasts. She sucked in a breath. "Virtuous—" she arched upward when his mouth replaced his hands "—saint-like—" she heard him chuckle at that one, then pay careful attention to her hardened nipple with his tongue "—wholesome…"

Unable to think any pure thoughts with Reese's hands

and mouth doing such exquisite things to her, unable to think at all, she simply joined him.

Streaks of light from the swiftly rising sun warmed the rumpled sheets by the time they collapsed in each other's arms, flushed with passion and breathing heavy.

He held her close, kissed her temple and cheek. "Who would have ever thought," he said, his voice husky and rough, "that Sydney Taylor was such a wanton woman?"

"Don't forget wicked," she murmured against his neck. "And loose and—"

"Sydney..."

She heard the shift in his voice from playful to serious, felt her heart stop, praying he would at least wait until later, or tomorrow, even, to tell her that last night had been a mistake.

"Tell me how a beautiful woman gets to the ripe old age of twenty-six without...well, why is it you never...that you were still..." He hesitated, obviously unsure how to phrase such a delicate question.

"A virgin?" she finished for him while relief poured through her that he hadn't said what she'd been thinking, and at the same time wondering why she wasn't mortified having this conversation with Reese. "Dating was never easy for me like it is for other women." She skimmed a restless finger over his chest. "And the longer I waited for the right man, the more difficult it became."

"You were engaged, Syd," Reese said gently. "To Bobby, of all people."

"I always thought that was why he asked me to marry him, because I wouldn't jump into bed with him the way most women did. Well, and because my family had money, too. Then after he did ask me to marry him,

I figured if I slept with him, he wouldn't want me anymore, money or not. I wanted to believe that, maybe just a little, Bobby really did love me."

Reese decided that if he ever saw Bobby again, he'd punch him in the nose. Just walk up and lay one on him, then walk away without so much as a second glance or thought. Thank God he hadn't married Sydney. She deserved much better than that muscle-brained moron.

And thank God she hadn't slept with the jerk, too. She definitely deserved better than Bobby in *that* department, as well. She deserved someone like...well, like himself, Reese thought. He cared about Sydney, respected and appreciated her. Which was more than Bobby had ever done.

And the fact that he'd been her first, Reese thought, made Sydney all the more special to him. Made him want to, well, beat his chest, as ridiculous as that sounded. She'd made him feel...virile. Powerful. Robust.

He had no idea how to tell her any of that, but suddenly he wanted to try. "Syd—"

She sat, pulled the sheet up to cover herself and shook her head. "Reese, the last thing in the world I want from you is pity. You don't have to tell me how absurd it was to believe that Bobby really wanted to marry me, or that he loved me. I know perfectly well how pathetic I was."

When he opened his mouth to protest, she put her fingers on his lips to silence him. "But that was the old Sydney Taylor," she said firmly. "I'm a new woman. In two weeks my restaurant will be open and now, thanks to you, I have an entirely different outlook on relationships."

"Which is?" The touch of her fingers on his mouth distracted him for a moment and he couldn't resist kissing each delicate fingertip, delighted at the shiver he felt ripple through her.

"You've been right all along, Reese. I'm much too serious about everything. Too analytical and uptight. It's time I learned how to relax and enjoy life more. Have more fun."

He smiled, moved his lips to the palm of her hand and kissed her there. "Atta girl, Syd."

"I have so much time to make up for." Her voice was breathless, her eyes bright. "So many new things to experience."

He was liking the sound of all this more and more. And he was just the man to help her out with all those new experiences, Reese thought cheerfully. Who was he to discourage such energetic enthusiasm?

Smiling, she let her head fall back and stretched her arms wide. "I feel so incredible."

She *looked* pretty damn incredible, too, Reese thought as the sheet slipped away from Sydney's breasts. He was reaching for her when she suddenly jumped out of bed. He took a moment to enjoy every naked curve, then realized she was pulling her clothes on.

"And just what do you think you're doing?" Lying on his side, he bent his elbow and propped his head in the palm of his hand. She looked tousled and sexy with her hair falling over her shoulders and her skin flushed from their lovemaking. He watched her pull on her bra and blouse, still amazed at the night they'd spent together.

The first of many, he thought with a smile.

"Have you seen my shoes?" She dropped to the

floor, and Reese's heart jumped at the momentary sight of her pretty lace-covered bottom thrust upwards as she looked under the bed. "Here they are."

That did it. He wanted her back in his bed. Right now. He reached out and dragged her up onto the mattress with him, then rolled her onto her back as he kissed her. "And just where do you think you're going?" he murmured as he nuzzled on her ear.

Her arms came over his shoulders. "Home, silly. It's getting late. You've got to get to work."

"What happened to all that talk about enjoying life and having more fun?" He trailed kisses down her neck, delighted in the soft little moan he heard from deep in her throat.

"Well, I wasn't just referring to making love, though that—" she sucked in a breath and arched upward as his hand cupped her breast "—is certainly pleasurable, too."

"So what did you mean?" He started to unbutton her blouse again.

"I meant life in general," she gasped softly, closed her eyes as his hand slid under her silk blouse. "Enjoying every moment. I've worried my entire life what people would think and say about me. I'm not going to do that anymore."

"Good." He frowned when she stilled his hand and pushed upward on his shoulders until they were both sitting. Okay. She wanted to talk, that was fine. He made a mental note where he'd left off, so he could be sure and come back to the right spot.

"You were right about me being a snob, Reese." She took his face in her hands and smiled. "But not anymore. I'm going to take the time to meet different kinds of people and do things I've never done before. Listen to rock music. Cut my hair. Buy a short skirt. Eat breakfast in bed. All the things I never allowed myself to do before.''

That all sounded great, especially the short skirt part. And she could eat breakfast in bed with him anytime. He'd even make it for her.

She didn't need to cut her hair, though. He liked it just the way it was. And come to think of it, if she wore a short skirt, other guys would be looking at those great legs of hers. He decided he didn't like that at all.

And what the hell did she mean about meeting different kinds of people?

Before he could ask her, she'd slipped out from underneath him, then grabbed her skirt from the floor and pulled it on. ''I don't want to make you late for work and I'm sure you wouldn't want to have to explain Sydney Taylor sneaking out of your place early in the morning looking like she'd slept in her clothes.''

He frowned at her. ''You just said you didn't care what people thought.''

She tugged on a shoe. ''I don't care what they think about me, but I wouldn't want you to have to endure any rib-poking or jokes because of me.''

''And you think *I* care what people think?'' Shaking his head in exasperation, he sat on the edge of the bed. ''And if just one person pokes my rib or even hints at making a joke, they'll be wearing their teeth.''

She went still, then looked at him with tear-filled eyes. ''That's the nicest thing anyone has ever said to me.'' She moved toward him, then lightly pressed her lips to his and said softly, ''Thank you, Reese. That was the most wonderful night of my life. You've been kind and honest and incredibly sweet. You made my first time special and I'll never forget that.''

Kind, honest and *sweet?* Never forget? What the hell was she talking about? He narrowed his eyes and frowned. "Is this a brush-off, Syd?"

"Of course not." She turned away, spotted her other shoe and reached for it. "But we're both responsible, mature adults, and I don't want you to think that I have any expectations regarding a continuing relationship. What happened last night just happened. I don't want you to feel any sense of...responsibility."

Responsibility? Would this woman ever cease to make him crazy?

Probably not.

"So what you're saying," he said carefully, "is that you just want to be friends. Is that it?"

Her cheeks flushed pink as her gaze met his. "Well...yes."

He didn't believe a word of what she was saying.

"Sure, Syd," he said easily. "We'll just be friends."

"Great." Smiling, she moved toward him. "These next few days are going to be busy getting ready for the café's opening, so I may not see you for a while."

"Okay."

"Bye." She brushed his cheek with her lips.

"Bye, Syd."

"Bye." She brushed his other cheek.

"Syd?"

"What?"

"Come back to bed."

He saw the relief in her eyes, then, with a laugh, she threw her arms around his neck and sent them both falling back on the mattress. "I thought you'd never ask."

# Nine

"**O**h, Lucian, it's so beautiful."

Sydney ran her hand over the new granite countertop that Lucian had just installed in the café. It would separate the dining area from the wine and beer and cappuccino machine on the back wall. If her tables were full, then customers could wait here on bar stools and have drinks or hors d'oeuvres until they were seated.

"It's strong enough to hold an elephant, too." Screwdriver in hand, Lucian knelt behind the countertop and gave the last screw head on the supporting cabinet a solid twist.

"I don't suppose I'll get too many elephants for customers," Sydney said lightly.

Lucian stood, slipped his screwdriver into the tool belt around his waist. "I suppose not. But there are Henry Offman's two teenage sons. Don't think I'd want those boys to come in any restaurant I owned. Some say they single-handedly shut down Barney's Buffet. Just be sure you don't have any All-You-Can-Eat nights or they'll clean you out.''

Laughing, she shook her head and joined him behind the counter. "How would you like to be my first cappuccino customer? Or maybe an espresso?''

"That's straight-up black, right? Whipped cream and foam on coffee is for wimps.''

"Espresso it is.''

He leaned against the counter and watched while she prepared the coffee. "Looks like you're just about ready to open.''

"Six days, four hours and thirty-two minutes.'' She handed him the aromatic dark coffee in a demitasse.

Lucian raised a skeptical brow at the miniature mug, then took a sip. "Not bad, Syd. By the way, I like your hair like that.''

"Thanks.'' Her cheeks warmed at the compliment. "I just got it cut this morning.''

Lucian's cell phone rang and while he spoke to his foreman regarding a building permit on a job site outside of town, Sydney glanced into the ceiling-high mirror behind the cappuccino machine. She still couldn't believe the woman looking back at her was Sydney Taylor.

It had taken her an entire week to work up the courage to go to the salon. She touched the sides of the shaggy, layered cut that Frederico had insisted was created just for her. He'd also talked her into adding a few highlights to her already blond hair, and while she had those silly pieces of foil in her hair, he handed her over to Marie, the esthetician, who'd tweaked and plucked, plastered mud on her face, then applied a light touch of eye make-up. By the time her hair had been blown dry, Sydney looked and felt like a new woman.

Marie had oohed and ahhed and nodded with approval.

Frederico had called her Sexy Sydney.

Sexy Sydney.

She smiled. No one had ever called her sexy in her entire life. She liked it.

She'd gone straight from the salon and bought that short skirt she'd told Reese last week she was going to buy, plus a few other items of clothing that she'd always admired on other women, but never thought right for herself.

She couldn't wait until Reese saw her in them.

Or not in them.

She felt her skin heat up at her lurid thoughts of Reese, what it felt like to have his hands on her, his mouth. They'd seen each other several times since they'd made love that first time. On Monday, when the tavern was closed, they'd gone for a drive through the back roads of the country to a lake where he told her that he and his brothers used to race cars and drink beer. Just thinking about how she and Reese had made love in a secluded glen by the lake made her heart quicken. Never in her wildest dreams would she have ever thought that she'd make love outside, surrounded by trees and bushes and the sky overhead.

With Reese Sinclair.

A woman couldn't ask for a more skilled, generous, thoughtful lover. One minute he was gentle, the next wild and rough. These past few days had been the most exciting time of her life. He'd come to her apartment one night after the tavern had closed, a bottle of wine in his hand. They drank it in her bed. And just yesterday afternoon he'd shown up while she was unpacking an order of bread baskets and dragged her over to his cottage. She'd been breathless, excited that he'd wanted to make love with her so much that he couldn't wait until that night.

But he hadn't wanted to make love. He'd wanted to show her his brand-new, just arrived off the UPS truck, first edition, signed copy of Hemmingway's *For Whom the Bell Tolls*.

The pleasure and excitement in his face had made her heart stutter. There was so much more to Reese Sinclair than she'd ever imagined, and the fact that he'd wanted to share something so special with her made her eyes tear.

Then she'd been the one kissing him, tugging his clothes off as she pulled him to his bed with an urgency that startled herself.

With a sigh, she turned back to the cappuccino machine and made herself a cup. She refused to think beyond the moment. She'd be a fool to think that there was any kind of future for her and Reese. She understood that their relationship—whatever it was—was not permanent. They were…dating. Sort of. Enjoying each other's company. Definitely. They took each day as it came. No commitments, no plans, no explanations.

And if she started to dream for a moment, let herself think for even a millisecond that there could be more, all she had to do was remember standing at the front of the church, forcing her knees not to give and her voice not to shake as she looked at all those people and made her excuses. The pity in everyone's eyes had nearly done her in. They'd seen all along what she'd been too blind to see. That Bobby had lied to the very end, made promises, told her he loved her and wanted her to be his wife. She didn't ever want to see that look in any-one's eyes again. She wouldn't be a fool again. This time she'd be realistic. No expectations.

But Reese was honest. He'd made no promises, and he'd certainly never told her that he loved her. As long as she didn't make a foolish mistake and fall in love with him, then she would survive when he decided to move on to the next woman.

She swallowed the sudden lump in her throat. She didn't want to think about that now. She wouldn't.

She turned suddenly and bumped into Lucian who'd just finished his call. He steadied her with one hand, then frowned at the coffee that had splashed over the side of her cup onto the front of her blue cotton sweater.

"Did it burn you?" he asked with concern.

"No, no, I'm fine." She grabbed a bar towel from a hook under the cappuccino machine and dabbed at the spot. "I've got it."

"You sure? I'd help you out, but then you might have to slap me. Course," he said, grinning at her with that same Sinclair smile that made women melt, "it might be worth it."

Laughing, she shook her head. The Sinclair men were all hopeless flirts, charming, but deadly. And Lucian, well, there was something under the surface with Lucian, something under that Sinclair smile and eyes that appeared wounded. She recognized that look. She'd seen it in her own eyes.

But she already had her hands full with one Sinclair male. She wasn't remotely interested in another.

That wasn't how it appeared to Reese, however, when he chose that moment to walk into the café. At the sight of his brother standing so close to Sydney behind the new countertop, with his hand on her arm, smiling at her and her smiling back, Reese's blood started to simmer.

"Can I get in on the joke, too?" He kept his gaze carefully on Lucian as he crossed the room. "Or is this just between you two?"

Startled, Sydney jumped, but Lucian turned smoothly and grinned.

"Hey, Reese." Lucian dropped his hand away from Sydney's arm and leaned back casually against the small counter that held the coffee machine. He took a slow, deliberate sip of his espresso. "What's up?"

"Not much." His gaze slid to Sydney, who had just enough guilt in her eyes to make his jaw tighten. And just what had she done to her hair? He looked back at Lucian. "What's up with you?"

"Just putting in the counter for Syd," he said easily, then raised the little cup in his hand. "I'm her first espresso customer."

"Is that right?" A muscle twitched in the corner of Reese's eye. He didn't want Lucian to be Sydney's first anything. Or any other guy for that matter. And he sure didn't like his brother standing behind that counter getting so cozy with his girl.

"Would you like a cup?" Sydney asked quickly and turned toward the machine. "It will just take a minute."

"Maybe if you put it in a real cup," Reese said evenly. "That little thing Lucian's got there won't do much to get the heart pumping."

Lucian raised a brow at his brother's dig. To say his name and "little thing" in the same breath were fighting words and they both knew it.

While Sydney worked the machine, Reese glared at his brother. Lucian grinned right back, sipping his coffee.

Reese took the cup that Sydney offered, was irritated that she seemed to be avoiding his gaze. "Ah, I've got to go soak this or the spot will never come out," she said hesitantly as she glanced down at the front of her sweater. "I'll be right back."

Reese noticed the coffee stain between her breasts, then narrowed his eyes as he realized that Lucian was looking at the same spot. When Sydney turned and walked out from behind the counter, Reese nearly spit out the coffee he'd just drank. She was wearing a tight, black skirt that didn't have enough fabric to wipe a tabletop dry. Her legs went on forever. So did Lucian's stare.

"Put your eyeballs back in your sockets and close your mouth," Reese growled after Sydney was gone.

"Did you get a look at those legs?" Lucian whistled softly. "Lord have mercy, I think I'm in love."

"Unless you want to eat that little cup in your hand," Reese warned, "don't say another word."

"Why, Reese," Lucian said with a smile, "I do believe you're jealous. Just say the word, Bro, and I'll back off."

"I'm not jealous," he snapped. "I never get jealous. But just touch her again, keep looking at her like that, or thinking what you're thinking, and you die."

"Well, well." Humor lit Lucian's eyes. "So you *do* have a thing for Sydney, don't you? We were all wondering where you'd been keeping yourself when you weren't at the tavern."

Reese had never come out and exactly announced that he and Sydney were seeing each other, but he had a right to a private life, didn't he? Who he saw or what he did was nobody's business but his own. "Sydney and I—'' he hesitated, trying to think of the right words ''—have an understanding.''

''Which is?''

''We like each other, enjoy each other's company.'' He took a sniff of the strong coffee, then sipped, decided he liked the strong, rich flavor. ''That's it.''

''Right.'' Lucian gave a snort of laughter. ''That's why you started barking and growling when you walked in and saw me with her. Because you *like* her.''

''That's right.''

''When I dated Susie Hutton at the same time you did, you never even blinked,'' Lucian said, obviously enjoying every minute of Reese's irritation. ''Or Mary Walinkski. She dumped you to go out with me and you didn't care. You liked them, didn't you?''

''I liked them *different*,'' he insisted. ''And Mary didn't dump me. I got busy and she got bored sitting around waiting for me to call. Anyway, Sydney is different, that's all.''

''Different from what?'' Sydney asked as she came back into the room, still wearing that little black skirt that had raised his blood pressure twenty notches and a V-neck pink sweater. It was all Reese could do not to grab the chef's apron laid over a bar stool and cover her up with it. Instead, he narrowed his eyes at Lucian, warning him off.

''Or should I say, different from who?'' Sydney handed a check to Lucian. ''Thanks, Lucian. The countertop is perfect.''

''Anytime you need anything,'' Lucian said smoothly, ''anything at all, Syd, just give me a call. You have my home number?''

Reese understood perfectly well that Lucian was goading him, but it still didn't ease the desire to grab his brother by the scruff of his neck and shove him out the door.

"That shouldn't be necessary." She smiled. "I'm sure I can find you if I need you."

Reese gritted his teeth, decided to rough his brother up later for setting him up like this.

"Thanks for the coffee." Lucian handed Sydney back the cup, slid a grin at Reese as he passed him. "See ya."

Reese nodded stiffly, watched Lucian stride casually out the front door, whistling as he stepped out into the cool November air.

"What did you mean, 'I'm different'?" Sydney asked, dragging Reese's attention from his brother back to her.

He moved toward her, backed her against the countertop and braced one arm on either side of her. He covered her mouth with his, felt a surge of hot satisfaction at the soft moan he heard rise from deep in her throat.

"Mmm," he murmured. "You taste like coffee and cream."

"Stop trying to distract me," she said, then slid her hands up his chest and gently nudged him away. "How am I different?"

"Your hair, for one thing. You cut it." He knew enough about women to never say you didn't like a new hairdo, but in this case he did like it. It made her eyes look bigger, her face softer. "Very sexy."

Pleasure shone in her blue eyes, and he felt something shift and move inside him, an unfamiliar tilt to his equilibrium that had him tightening his grip on the countertop to steady himself. Lack of sleep, he decided.

He hadn't had much of that this past week, between making love at night with Sydney, or wanting to.

"That's what Frederico said," she said, her voice breathy.

"Who?"

"The stylist who cut my hair."

"Oh." He felt the tension ease from his shoulders. "I was beginning to think I was going to have to beat up every guy in town, including Lucian."

Especially Lucian, he thought, remembering the way his brother had drooled over Sydney's legs.

"Reese, Frederico is a happily married man, with two children." She laughed at the surprise on his face. "And *Lucian?* You're actually jealous of your own brother?"

There was that damn word again. "Protective," he said, deciding he liked the neutrality of that word.

"Of me?" She stared at him in wide-eyed wonder. "Why?"

"Why wouldn't I be?" he asked irritably, uncomfortable with the shift this conversation had taken. Why did women have to make things so complicated? Pick every thought and word apart and analyze it?

"Well…" Her gaze dropped to his chest while she busied one fingertip circling a button on his denim shirt. "I realize that we're sleeping together, but I never—"

"Just stop right there."

He took hold of her arms, narrowed his eyes as he looked down at her startled face.

"We're not just *sleeping together,*" he said through clenched teeth, then eased up on the tight grip he had on her. "I think I deserve better than a comment like that, and so do you."

"Okay. I'm sorry." Her fingers stilled, then she

asked carefully, "So what are we doing, then?" she asked carefully.

Oh, hell. Too many damn questions, when all he wanted to do was drag her upstairs to her apartment and make wild love with her all afternoon. "We're...seeing each other, Syd. Exclusively. In spite of what you may have heard about me, I'm not with a different woman every night and while I may not be a saint, I sure as hell haven't slept with all the ones I have gone out with. Not even close. Got that?"

He'd never explained himself to any woman before, Reese realized with annoyance. It surprised him, as much as it aggravated him, that he felt the need to do so now.

"All right." She spread her fingers on his chest, her expression thoughtful. "So you like my new haircut?"

His annoyance dissolved, in its place a heat built where her fingers had begun to move over his chest. "Yeah, I do. And you know what else I like?"

"What?" She leaned forward and pressed her lips to his throat.

"This skirt." His pulse quickened when she nipped lightly at the base of his throat. "I especially like this skirt."

His hands slid the fabric up and slipped underneath to reveal the tiniest sliver of black satin. He moaned softly, reached behind her and cupped her firm buttocks, lifted her up to fit snugly against the growing ache in the front of his jeans.

"I was hoping you would," she murmured, slipping her arms around his neck and pressing herself even closer, moving her hips in a way that made his heart slam like a fist in his chest.

He'd never wanted a woman the way he wanted her,

didn't understand the need that rocked him to his very core. Didn't want to understand it.

Right now, he only understood the urgency racing through his veins to possess her completely, thoroughly, mindlessly.

He scooped her up in his arms and carried her upstairs to her tidy, organized apartment, laid her down on her feather mattress, felt the last of his control snap when she held out her arms to him and pulled him down beside her.

"Just for the record," she said, gasping when he pushed her skirt up around her waist, "I'm not interested in Lucian."

"Sydney—" he skimmed the edge of her panties with one curious fingertip, felt masculine satisfaction at the sound of her sharp intake of breath and the upward thrust of her hips "—I don't want to talk about my brother right now."

"Okay." The blue of her eyes darkened with desire when he palmed the soft mound between her legs. She moved against his hand, closed her eyes on a moan. "What shall we talk about? The weather?"

"I heard there's a storm coming in." Just watching her squirm underneath him set Reese's blood boiling. He moved over her, inched her sweater upward with one hand while he caressed her intimately with the other. "You might want to stay inside to keep warm."

"Maybe I should light a fire." She sucked in a breath when his hand closed over her breast.

"I'll do it."

He slipped his hand under the band of elastic on her panties, then slid into the damp heat of her body and moved in a time-old rhythm, letting her set the pace. She arched upward when he leaned down and kissed her belly, raked her hands through his hair, grasping at his shoulders while his mouth moved lower.

"Reese," his name was ragged on her lips, a frantic plea.

He took his time, nuzzling the sensitive flesh on the inside of her thighs, softly biting, teasing with his mouth, stroking, loving her.

When she surged upward, gasping, then melted bonelessly back onto the soft mattress, he quickly slid her panties off, still kissing her while he tugged his jeans down. She opened to him, drew him to her. He heard her name on his lips as he drove himself deep inside her, heard the sound of his own hoarse breathing and her soft encouragement.

Insanity, he thought, as his body coiled tighter and tighter. What her hands did to him, her mouth. He looked at her, thought her the most beautiful, exciting woman he'd ever seen. Her eyes, glazed with passion, met his hard gaze; her lips, softly parted and swollen from his kisses, whispered his name.

Pure insanity.

And then he did go crazy, completely, and took her with him.

# Ten

The snowstorm hit exactly as Reese had predicted, only three days later. Three days after that and twelve inches later, snow was still falling lightly on Bloomfield County; a pretty picture of white that covered roofs and cars and roads. On any other day Sydney would have appreciated the softly falling flakes and peacefulness. She might have put on her boots and gone for a walk, sat in front of a fire and sipped a hot brandy. Read a good book.

Any other day but today.

Today was the grand opening of Le Petit Bistro.

She stood at the window of the café in her new white silk suit, stared out at the snow-covered roads and walks. Her heart sank at the sight of the empty streets. Very few people came out on an evening like this, those that did had a purpose or a need. They didn't usually go out to dinner, especially to French restaurants with pink linen tablecloths and cappuccino machines.

Turning from the window, she scanned the restaurant; candles flickered softly from crystal-cut votives, one fresh pink rose bud on every table, strains of Mozart floating from the sound system. The scent of garlic and herbs filled the room. Everything looked exactly as she'd pictured in her mind.

Well, not exactly. In her mind, there'd also been customers.

The few reservations that had been made had been cancelled earlier in the day, but she'd still hoped until the last minute that the snow would stop and bring people out of their homes. When it hadn't, she'd simply hoped that people would come out anyway. The roads were still drivable, and the temperature wasn't as cold as it had been the past two days.

But she'd been open for business exactly twenty-two minutes and so far, her front door hadn't opened once. Her own grandfather wasn't even coming. He'd been snowed in at Baltimore airport and wouldn't be back until tomorrow. And Reese had his own business to run, with a short staff to run it. He had told her he'd come by, but he hadn't said when. If his place was as slow as hers was, she guessed he'd be by in an hour or two, but she knew that in this weather, people would be much more inclined to go out for a casual dinner and a beer than a fancy French meal.

There would be other days, of course. People would come once the snow stopped, she was certain of that. But this day, the first day, was special. A person always remembered firsts, she thought, and touched one soft petal of the pink rose on the table beside her. In spite of everything, she felt herself smile.

When she thought of firsts, Reese instantly came to mind.

But then, he was on her mind most of the time. She'd been too busy this past week taking care of all the last minute preparations to see him. Well, except for two nights ago, when he'd called late at night just to say hello, and the conversation escalated into a scintillating discussion of what she was wearing. As she'd laid back in her bed to describe her pink satin nightie in detail, a knock at her door interrupted her. It was Reese, out of breath from his sprint across the street. The second she'd opened the door he'd pulled her into his arms and made love to her right there, standing against the door he'd kicked closed.

Just thinking about the intensity in his dark eyes, the way he'd lifted her off the floor and she'd wrapped her legs around his waist, made her pulse quicken and her skin heat up.

"Ms. Taylor? Is there anything else you want me to do while we're waiting? I already folded the napkins."

Sydney glanced over her shoulder at Becky, her hostess, and smiled. "Why don't I show you how the cappuccino machine works? When Nell and I get busy with orders and serving, we may need you to fill in for us." *Hope springs eternal,* she thought with a sigh.

"Did I hear my name?" Nell popped her head out from the kitchen and glanced around. "Please tell me we've got customers. Latona has made a crab cake in some kind of sauce that could bring a grown man to his knees."

Sydney had worked all week with Latona fine-tuning all the recipes for the café. Most were Sydney's creations, but what her chef could do with pasta and chicken bordered on genius.

At the sound of the front door opening, all three heads turned expectantly.

Sydney's heart sank. It was a man wearing a mechanic's uniform and a baseball cap. "Anybody here call for a tow?" he barked.

Sydney shook her head, considered dragging the man inside and forcing him to sit at one of her tables. He was a lot bigger than her, but she was determined enough she could probably wrestle him into a chair.

Fifteen minutes later, with the snow still softly falling and not one customer in sight, she smoothed the corners of each table for the tenth time while Becky practiced making cappuccinos and Nell received an impromptu cooking lesson in the kitchen from Latona.

The door opened again.

A customer. A living, breathing customer.

Well, at least, sort of. It was Griswald Mantle, who'd had his eightieth birthday party last week at the tavern. His wife had passed on last year, and he spent most of his time at the tavern now.

For a moment Sydney thought maybe he was confused and had mistakenly walked into the wrong place, but he shuffled directly to a table without even waiting for a flustered Becky to seat him, handed her his coat, then sat, tucked his napkin into his shirt and asked for some bread.

Well, it was a beginning, Sydney thought and started toward his table to welcome him. Then the door opened again. This time it was Margaret and Jimmy Metzer, who owned the dry cleaners three stores down. Sydney seated them while Nell brought a basket of bread for Griswald.

Pandemonium struck five minutes later when the Sinclair-Shawnessey clan arrived. Cara and Ian, Callan and Abby, Gabe and Melanie and Kevin.

"Sorry we're late." Cara unwrapped the scarf from around her neck and shook the snow from her hair. "The roads slowed us a bit. Oh, Sydney, this is so beautiful."

"You shouldn't have come out in this weather." But she couldn't help being pleased that they all had. While Sydney hung their coats on the rack inside the door, Becky and Nell hurried about with breadbaskets and water glasses.

Lucian showed up next with Louise Wittmeyer on his arm, the pretty brunette office manager from Do-Right Lumber; Ken and Jan Stockton, local horse ranchers came in after them.

And so it went. They trickled in, shrugging out of coats and hats, filling the tables that had been empty just a short time ago. Sydney offered free samples of hors d'oeuvres and champagne, while Nell took orders and Becky helped serve.

For the first time in her life, Sydney felt completely alive. Whole. As she bustled about, she watched her customers enjoy the food she'd prepared, smile and roll their eyes with approval, and her chest swelled with joy.

And then Reese walked in.

Her hand tightened on the unopened bottle of wine she'd just removed from the rack under the countertop; she sucked in a breath at the sight of him. Flakes of snow dusted his dark hair and the shoulders of his brown leather bomber jacket. His gaze scanned the room, then stopped when he saw her.

He smiled.

Her heart skipped, then raced.

Never mind the room was crowded, filled with the

sounds of people talking and enjoying a meal, and that she was supposed to be serving her customers. Suddenly the only two people in the world were Reese and herself.

And then she simply knew.

She loved him.

She supposed at some level she'd known that she loved him since that first time he'd taken her to his bed. No, before that, she admitted to herself. When she'd hit him in the nose with that door then held his face in her hands and looked into those amazing eyes of his, that's when she'd really known.

But she'd refused to accept it, and even after they'd made love, she'd told herself she could handle their relationship without letting her heart get involved. The "new" Sydney wasn't looking for a commitment, she'd convinced herself. A man like Reese didn't play for keeps, he simply played, enjoyed the moment and the woman he was with at the time.

Well, the "new" Sydney was just as big a fool as the "old" Sydney. She'd fallen in love with a man who would never love her back the way she wanted. The way she needed.

Or could he?

The way he looked at her right now, as if she were the most beautiful woman, the *only* woman in the room—in the world—made her hope for things she shouldn't hope for. That she didn't dare hope for.

His gaze slid away then, looked at Becky who was staring at him as if he were a giant ice-cream cone she'd like to gobble up. He had that affect on women, Sydney knew, herself included. Only she thought of him as a potato chip and she wanted the whole bag. Every last, tasty morsel.

He shrugged out of his jacket and moved toward her then, still smiling, his intense gaze locked on hers. He looked incredibly handsome in a dark blue dress shirt, new jeans and—good Heavens, she never thought she'd see it—a tie.

"Congratulations, Ms. Taylor. Le Petit Bistro is a hit." He took her hand, brought it to his mouth. His compliment, as well as the touch of his warm lips on her suddenly cold fingers made her breath catch.

"You made it." She smiled at him, pushed away all the worry and doubt and just let herself enjoy. "Can you stay for a while?"

"The burners are out at the tavern, and we were slow anyway because of the storm. I decided to close down."

She should feel bad that he'd had to close down his business, but she was thrilled. "You mean I have you for the night?"

He kept her hand to his mouth, discreetly touched the tip of his tongue to her knuckle. "All night," he whispered, his voice heavy with promise.

"*All* night?" She raised a brow. "That's an ambitious endeavor, Mr. Sinclair. Are you sure you're feeling up for it?"

He gave her a wicked grin. "I'm certain I will be."

Heat shivered up her arm. "I set a place for you at your family's table, just in case you made it," she said softly. "But I'm busier than I expected so I may not be able to give you as much personal attention as I'd hoped."

"You can make up for it later, darlin'. In fact—" he kissed her hand again, nibbled this time "—I'm counting on your *very* personal attention."

The glint in Reese's eyes made Sydney's heart pound. With a wink, he walked away and joined his family. She stared after him, reminded herself to breathe. Lord, but the man was a distraction, she thought with a smile. A wonderful, sexy, exciting distraction.

"Table four would like a glass of Merlot," Nell said as she breezed by with an order. "A diet soda at six and more bread at seven."

Sydney snapped her attention back to her work, poured the wine and soda, filled a new breadbasket, then carefully composed herself. After all, she thought with a grin, a full-grown woman skipping around an elegant restaurant serving food and drink would hardly be considered dignified, now, would it?

"Get the wheelbarrow now and wheel me out." Cara sat back in her chair with a satisfied groan, but still had her eyes on the last bite of chocolate éclair on her husband's dessert plate.

"Good thing you've got those expanding pants," Ian said playfully. "I wouldn't want our son to get too crowded in there."

Cara placed a hand on her stomach and smiled. "Look who's talking. You ate an apple tart *and* an éclair."

"I couldn't very well hurt Sydney's feelings when she brought me an éclair on the house, could I?" And to make sure he didn't, he finished the last bite, then sighed with delight.

"We'd all be as big as houses if we ate like this every day." Melanie pushed her own plate away. "I couldn't force another bite."

"Maybe that's because you don't have another bite left," Gabe teased, then pulled a sleepy Kevin onto his lap and smoothed his rumpled sandy-blond hair.

"Sydney says she's open for lunch on Thursdays and Fridays," Abby said, still working on her own éclair. "Why don't we come here after our dress fittings on Thursday?"

The ladies all agreed, then Cara looked at Reese. "By the way, one of the males sitting at this table hasn't gone in for their tux fitting yet."

Callan, Ian and Gabe all looked at Reese. Good grief, he thought, sinking in his chair, it was bad enough he'd put this noose called a tie around his neck tonight. Just the thought of wearing that monkey suit made his neck itch.

"Monday," he promised reluctantly, though he'd already planned on spending his day off with Sydney. Somewhere quiet and extremely private.

When the conversation between the ladies shifted to talk about the wedding, seats were rearranged, separating ladies from men. While Gabe and Ian argued over the last Eagles-Cowboys game, Reese only half-listened as he scanned the café, hoping for a glimpse of Sydney. He narrowed his eyes at the sight of her serving wine to Mary Lou and Rhonda, who had come into the café with Emmett and Dean Farley, brothers who owned twenty acres of farmland just outside of town. Reese didn't like the idea of Sydney waiting on the women after what they'd said about her. But Sydney was smiling and talking to them as if nothing had ever happened, so she must have let it go. Or was at least pretending that she had.

His gut still twisted every time he remembered how she'd cried that night. He'd rather walk barefoot over broken glass than see her cry like that again.

He didn't know what she was doing to him, but he didn't like it one little bit.

When he wasn't with her, he spent hours thinking about her. When he was with her, all he could think about—other than making love to her—was when he would see her again.

He'd never done that with a woman before. Never wondered what she was doing when he wasn't with her, or if she was thinking about him. If she was listening to the same song on the radio, maybe looking at the phone thinking she should call.

She was driving him absolutely crazy.

Maybe he should back off, he thought. Let things cool a little between them. Get his head on straight so he could think more clearly about them, about their relationship. Just the thought of that word and what it might mean had him slipping a finger under the knot of his tie and loosening it.

Still, he watched her move about the restaurant, this new Sydney, who was softer, sweeter, more approachable. This was her night to shine and she was, literally. Her face glowed with pleasure, her eyes sparkled; it was all he could do not to drag her upstairs right now and make love to her. He glanced at his watch, figured he'd have to wait a couple of hours before he could manage to entice her away. And when he did, he was going to slowly strip that pretty silk suit off her, take his time as he opened every pearl button on her jacket, slide his hands inside—

Realizing where his thoughts had gone and where he was, he caught himself, blinked, then turned back to the table.

Gabe, Ian, Callan all stared at him, grinning like idiots. "What?" He wiped at his mouth.

"Either he's got a bad case of indigestion or he's in

love.'' Callan draped his arms over the back of his chair.

''They're pretty much the same,'' Gabe said knowingly. ''But the way he's looking at Sydney, I'd put five bucks down that says it's love.''

Reese shook his head and grinned right back at them. ''Don't count me in your little club of hearts and flowers, boys. This Sinclair is made of tougher stuff than that.''

''He's hooked.'' Ian slapped a five-dollar bill on the table.

''Big time.'' Callan did the same.

After the amazing meal that Reese had just eaten, he was too relaxed and satisfied to argue with anyone. Besides, it required patience when dealing with fools. ''We're two adults enjoying each other's company, that's all,'' he said easily.

''Well, we know Sydney is one of the adults,'' Callan said. ''So who's the other?''

''Didn't you guys know?'' Lucian slipped into the chair where Kevin had been sitting. ''Reese told me that he and Sydney have an understanding.''

Reese frowned at his brother, deciding he would definitely have to beat him up later. ''I thought you had a date. She get scared off already by that ugly face of yours?''

''She's in the powder room.'' Never one to let an opportunity pass to rile up a brother, Lucian leaned back in his chair and grinned. ''You married guys all know the understanding. Whatever the woman says is the way it is, they insist you pick out rings and china together, only she decides what you'll buy, that—''

''What are you men talking about?'' Frowning, Cara cut in. All the women were listening now.

"Lucian was just giving us his opinions on marriage," Reese said easily. "I'm sure he wouldn't mind repeating them for you."

The women all looked at Lucian, who was smart enough about the female gender to know it was time to get outta Dodge. "Oops, my date's back. Gotta go."

Enjoying himself, Reese reached for the beer he'd been working on for the past hour, keeping an eye on the kitchen door that he'd seen Sydney go through a few minutes ago. The crowd had thinned out and he knew that she would be closing soon. He'd already decided he'd help her clean up and shut down so they could have their own private celebration of her opening night success.

In fact, no reason not to get started now, he thought, anxious to get Sydney alone. He mumbled a goodbye to his family, then headed for the kitchen.

"Reese Sinclair. There you are, you little devil."

Groaning silently, Reese found himself face-to-face with Mary Lou. Coming from the restroom, she wobbled toward him on four-inch heels, her eyes glazed over. Rhonda was with her, but she held back, obviously uncomfortable.

He looked for a way out, but the women were between him and the kitchen. He glanced back over his shoulder at his family, hoping for some help from that corner, but they were all busy talking.

Damn.

"Mary Lou. Rhonda." He didn't smile, but good manners kept him from ignoring them completely. "Excuse me."

"Anytime you wanna play poker with me, honey," Mary Lou said, slowly running one long red fingernail down the front of his tie, "just call. I won't even care if you cheat to win."

Reese went very still, refrained from slapping her hand away. "You better get back to your table, Mary Lou. Emmett and Dean are waiting."

Rhonda tugged on her friend's arm. "Let's go, Mary Lou."

"Oh, come on, Reese," Mary Lou said, slurring her words. "Don't pretend you don't know what I'm talking about. Marilyn told me she heard you tell Lucian that you and Sydney Taylor played poker because of your dog digging up her stupid flowers, and that you cheated to win just to knock her off that high horse of hers."

Reese glanced at the kitchen door, thankful that Sydney hadn't come back out, then looked over his shoulder at Emmett and Dean, relieved when he saw them getting out of their chairs, looking embarrassed by Mary Lou's rising voice. "You're drunk," he said tightly.

"What a man won't do to get a girl in bed." Mary Lou laughed, and her voice rose even higher. "So, you into charity work these days, Reese? I'm sure Sydney was grateful for your philanthropic service, but—Hey!"

Emmett grabbed hold of Mary Lou's arm and practically dragged her toward the front door, while Dean and Rhonda hurried behind, gathering jackets.

Reese drew in a slow breath to calm the anger pumping through him, then realized that the restaurant had gone quiet.

The few customers who were still in the restaurant were staring, not at him, but past him. *Oh, God, no.*

He saw her standing behind the countertop, where she'd been kneeling. A wine bottle still in her hand, she stared blankly at him, her face pale. She'd heard every damn word.

"You cheated?" she whispered so softly he could barely hear her. "Just to teach me a lesson?"

Panic slammed in his chest. "No, Syd, it wasn't like that—"

"You made me work for you, shell those stupid peanuts, then you actually let me believe that you—" She stopped, sucked in a breath, then smiled stiffly. "That's a pretty good one, Sinclair. You must be some kind of hero around here, playing a joke like that on me, of all people. I gotta hand it to you, you are smooth."

"Dammit, Sydney, will you just let me—"

"No, Reese." Carefully, she set the wine bottle down. "I won't let you."

She turned smooth as silk and walked back into the kitchen. He started to follow, but Nell blocked the doorway, her eyes narrowed and accusing. He considered picking her up and moving her, but realized if he touched the woman, he'd probably have assault added to his already long list of evil doings.

He'd give her a little time to calm down. She'd understand once he explained what had really happened. That it hadn't been the way Mary Lou said.

At least, not exactly.

Knowing that every female in the room would probably like to stick their butter knife in his back—including his own sister—he opted for retreat.

On an oath, he grabbed his jacket, stalked out of the restaurant and didn't look back.

# Eleven

"**T**en pounds of shrimp...twenty pounds of white fish...ten filets..."

Pen in hand, Sydney sat at the counter and entered the items Nell recited onto her shopping list, pausing here and there to make adjustments on quantities. She'd be opening at eleven-thirty today, and she'd offered discounts, plus free desserts to all the employees of local businesses to come in at lunchtime.

Her dream had come true.

She'd been in business exactly six days, not counting Monday when she'd closed, and the café, so far at least, was a success. Her customers loved the food and atmosphere, not to mention the reasonable prices, and she was already booked for the weekend prime dinner hours.

She should be dancing on this countertop Lucian put

in, swinging from the chandelier, swigging champagne and laughing.

She wanted to cry.

She wouldn't, of course. Not even for Reese would she let herself crumble into a pathetic little pile and bawl like a baby. She wanted to, but she refused to let the pain take control. Refused to let a broken heart turn her into some weepy, maudlin female. She would despise herself, and Reese, too, if she fell apart. In spite of what he'd done, the fool he'd made out of her, she couldn't hate him. It would only be another lie to deny that she loved him, that she always would.

She hadn't answered any of the messages he'd left every day on the answering machine in her apartment, and when he'd called the café, she'd been polite, then told him she was busy and she'd call him back, but didn't.

Over time the pain would ease, she'd been there enough times to know that. She might take longer to heal this time, but she would. She had to.

At least she had the café to keep her busy, occupy her mind and hands so she wouldn't think about him every minute of every day...every night...

"—six thousand pounds of pickled porcupine, five thousand pounds mongoose medallions, ten tubs of turtles—"

"What?" Sydney glanced up. "Turtles?"

Nell folded her arms and leaned across the counter. "Sydney, why don't you call him?"

"Call who?" She glanced back at her list and studied it as if it were a difficult algebraic problem.

Nell pulled the list from Sydney's stiff hand. "He's called and sent flowers every day, Syd."

Sydney glanced at the huge vase of red roses that had

just arrived. She allowed herself a moment to appreciate their beauty, then shook her head. "These are going back, just like the others," she said firmly.

A man had finally sent her flowers and she was sending them back. Funny how life worked out that way. Hilarious.

Nell shrugged. "Maybe you should just listen to what he has to say."

"Maybe you should."

Reese.

Her heart jumped at the sound of his voice. *Slow breaths,* she told herself. Slow, calming breaths.

Shoulders squared, she glanced over her shoulder at him.

He stood at the open door, watching her, his expression dark and somber. It pleased her that he looked a little ragged around the edges, but she supposed a guilty conscience did that to a person.

She'd known that she'd have to face him sooner or later. They lived and worked on the same street, in a town that wasn't all that big. "Good morning, Reese." She offered a stiff smile. "What can I do for you?"

Reese slid a look at Nell, who sighed, then shook her head as she headed back to the kitchen. "I'll go place this order, Syd. You still want those turtles?"

"That won't be necessary."

Reese frowned at the strange request, but he obviously had other things on his mind than Nell and turtles. He moved toward her, his jaw clenched tight. "You haven't called me."

"I apologize." Needing distance between her and Reese as much as needing something to do with her hands, she slid off the stool she'd been sitting on, moved behind the countertop and reached for the container of coffee she'd ground fresh a little while ago. "I've been busy here."

"We need to talk about this, Syd."

"All right." She scooped the grounds into the basket, but lost count. She'd be damned if she'd recount in front of Reese. "I have about five minutes before I have to set up for lunch today."

"Dammit, Sydney." He raked a hand through his dark hair. "You owe me more than five minutes."

She arched one brow, looked coolly at him as she flipped on the coffee machine. "We don't owe each other a thing, Reese. We had fun for a few days, that's all."

Like a caged cat, he began to pace. "Look, I know you're upset because of what Mary Lou said the other night. I'm sorry about that. If you'll just let me explain, we can—"

"Did you—" she cut him off "—or did you not cheat when we played poker, with the intention of, and I quote, 'knocking me off my high horse'?"

"Well, sort of, but—"

"I suppose there were side bets going on how long I'd tough it out working at the tavern." She reached for a towel, wiped at the counter. "Then, of course, there'd certainly be bets on how long it would take you to get me into bed. You must have made a pretty penny there."

He moved on her so fast she didn't even see him coming. One second she was wiping up some spilled grounds on the counter, the next second he had his hands on her arms and was holding her up against his body.

"Don't say that." His face was tight with anger.

"Don't ever say that. What happened between us wasn't planned, and it sure as hell was mutual."

His anger surprised her, but she refused to let him intimidate her, or get through her defenses ever again. "You're right, of course. Just because people like Mary Lou believe it's true, well, what difference does it make what they think? So what if they have a few laughs at my expense? I can live with that." She had lived with it for years. She'd survive.

Somehow, she'd survive.

A muscle jumped in his temple, but he slowly loosened his hold on her. "Other than I'm sorry, I don't know what to say. Tell me what to say, Syd."

Knowing he would never say the words she wanted to hear, she simply sighed. "A few flowers and 'I'm sorry's' won't make it okay, Reese," she said softly, then drew in a breath to steady herself. "But I would like to put all this behind us and still be friends."

"Friends?" Startled, he dropped his hands away from her. "You want to be friends?"

"If that's all right with you."

A glint of something dark and primal shone in his eyes, then it was gone, as if a shade had been drawn. "Sure," he said tightly. "Friends."

"Good." She managed to force a smile, even though her heart was shattering slowly into tiny, jagged little pieces. She turned away from him and wiped at the counter again. "If you'll excuse me now, I've got a hundred things to do. You know how it is in this business."

"Yeah. I know how it is."

He turned, started for the door.

"Reese?"

He stopped, glanced over his shoulder.

"Did...did your family all know about what happened, I mean, before?"

"Just Lucian, only because he guessed."

She closed her eyes with relief. She didn't know how she would have managed, how she'd ever face them again, if they'd all known and had been laughing at her.

She nodded, but didn't say anything. She felt his hesitation, and it frightened her. If he didn't leave, she was certain she would crumple up into a little ball.

But then she heard the door close behind him. She let out the breath she'd been holding, then leaned against the counter for support. She hadn't thought it possible to hurt any more than she already was.

But once again, she'd been wrong.

So very, very wrong.

A wedding was just as good a reason as any to get drunk, Reese decided. And since it was his own brother's wedding, so much the better. Nobody would question him if he got plastered and made a fool out of himself.

Something he seemed to be very good at these days.

Frowning, he stared at the beer in his hand, then took a big swig and leaned back in his chair to watch the reception guests dance to "Livin' La Vida Loca." Normally he'd be out there, too, celebrating and having a good time, but tonight the only celebrating he intended to do was with a bottle. He'd pay for it tomorrow, but for a few hours tonight, at least, he could forget about a curvy blue-eyed blonde with skin like silk and a mouth that could make a man groan out loud. He listened to the music and decided the number should be his theme song.

Living the Crazy Life. That was him all right.

Only Sydney could make a man crazy like that, he thought and threw back another slug of beer. Make a man wake up in the middle of the night, his sheets tangled and damp with sweat. Intrude into every tiny corner of his life, every thought, until there wasn't anything else but her. The sound of her laugh, the smell of her skin, the feel of her body against his.

His hand tightened on the bottle.

Dammit, he couldn't even get drunk without her invading his mind.

What else could he say to her that he hadn't already said? Before he'd finally gone over there to talk to her last week, he'd apologized a dozen times, sent flowers. He didn't know what else to do.

*A few flowers and I'm sorry's won't make it okay,* she'd told him.

So what the hell would?

Well, fine, then. He certainly wasn't going to crawl after her. He'd get over it, get over her.

He took another long pull on his beer. He would, dammit.

"Well, well, what have we here? Somebody looks lonely."

Reese frowned at Lucian and Callan, who'd just come off the dance floor and grabbed a beer on their way to harass him. When they turned two chairs around and straddled them, he knew they were settling in for a while. He'd get up and leave, but since they'd just follow, he didn't much see the point.

"He's still pining for Sydney," Callan said to Lucian.

"I'm not pining for anyone," Reese growled.

Lucian laughed. "Right. That's why you've been

holed up in the tavern for two weeks and you've been snapping at everyone who even looks at you.''

''I haven't snapped at anyone,'' Reese snapped.

''It's not as if we don't understand, Bro.'' Lucian tipped his beer to his lips. ''I mean, Sydney's a fine-looking woman, especially since she did that thing to her hair and started wearing those short skirts and sweaters. I saw her yesterday at the post office and she had on the hottest little—''

''Shut up, Lucian.'' Reese slammed his bottle down on the table. Dammit, his brothers had even spoiled his taste for beer. ''Just shut up.''

The beer bottle that had been halfway to Lucian's mouth stopped. ''Course, she looks fine in a slinky black dress and high heels, too. Damn fine.''

Reese followed Lucian's gaze across the crowded reception room. His heart stopped, then slammed against his ribs.

Sydney.

Her dress had a scoop neck, long sleeves and flared softly around her knees. Legs that never seemed to end were encased in black stockings; her high heels were spiked; her hair pulled up in a fountain of curls that cascaded down her slender neck. She stood with Melanie and Gabe, smiling as she congratulated them on their marriage. When Gabe kissed her, Reese felt his insides twist.

''Wow.''

It took Reese a moment to realize that Lucian had said the word out loud and not himself. ''Wow'' definitely described her.

''What's she doing here?'' Reese asked, surprised that his tongue still worked.

''Melanie asked her to come.'' Callan sat back with

a grin on his face. "When the women went into her café for lunch the week before last, they all bullied her until she promised to at least come to the reception for a little while."

It figured that no one would tell him. He'd been a pariah with the females in his family since the Mary Lou incident. Cara had chewed him out big time for his stupidity; Melanie and Abby had been silent, but the accusation in their eyes stung. As if he needed anyone to tell him what an idiot he'd been.

Lucian set his beer down and started to rise. "Since you're not pining for her, Bro, then I'm sure you won't mind if I—"

"Take one step toward her and you'll be wearing that cummerbund around your neck."

Lucian sighed, then shrugged and sat back down. "Let me know if you change your mind."

Keeping his eyes on Sydney, Reese stood and made his way across the room. He was probably just making a bigger fool out of himself than he already was, if that were possible, but what the hell?

"Dance?" he asked from behind her.

Her red lips thinned as she turned. "No, thank you, I—"

"We're friends, remember? Friends can dance together."

Ignoring her resistance, he pulled her into his arms and led her out onto the floor. He said a silent prayer of thanks when the music changed from fast to slow, a popular song by a current group about needing someone tonight. He pulled her close, felt her stiffen.

"You look good, Syd." She felt good, too. And her perfume was different tonight, he realized. Something exotic and sexy, intended to drive a man crazy. Not that she needed perfume for that. He was already there.

"Thank you." She placed a hand between them, eased back. "You look nice, too. If you'll excuse me, I really need to go see—"

"How did you manage to get off work?" He figured if he kept the conversation more business oriented, she wouldn't run off as quickly.

"I hired one new waitress and Nell's sister is in town for a few days. She manages a delicatessen in New York and offered to help out at the café tonight."

He hated the cool, disinterested tone in her voice. She wasn't disinterested, dammit. He *knew* she wasn't.

Or, fool that he was, maybe he was just hoping.

"That woman Lucian is dancing with," she asked casually, "who is she?"

If she was trying to twist the knife in his gut, she was doing a hell of a job, Reese thought as he narrowed his gaze at his brother, then back at her. "That's Raina, Melanie's maid-of-honor," he said tightly.

"I thought she looked familiar," Sydney said thoughtfully. "She came into the café on Thursday night with Melanie."

A tiny bit of the tension that had gathered in his shoulders eased as he realized she wasn't thinking about Lucian, but Raina. Reese had met the pretty brunette last night at the rehearsal dinner, but had been too caught up with thoughts of Sydney to even consider wandering into that territory. He'd thought at first that Lucian had been interested in Melanie's friend, but the way she and Lucian had avoided each other after their initial meeting, Reese figured that he'd been wrong about any attraction between the two. If anything, he thought, watching the stiff way they moved around the dance floor together and the expressions on their faces, they looked as if they'd rather dance with an axe murderer than each other.

Reese made a mental note to tweak Lucian's pin later over the woman's rejection. Payback's a bitch, dear brother, Reese thought with a smile.

Ian and Cara danced past them at that moment and said hello to Sydney, then Callan and Abby came by next. Reese wanted to be alone with Sydney, away from this crowd and the prying eyes of his family. He was certain she hadn't meant what she'd said about being friends with him. If she would just talk to him, he could change her mind. He knew he could. He just had to keep her in his arms long enough for her to relax a little, to remind her how good it had been between them.

Weather was a neutral subject, he decided. She didn't have to run from that topic. "It's supposed to snow again tonight."

"That's what I heard."

"Maybe tomorrow, too."

"Should be lovely."

Okay, well, maybe weather wasn't the best topic, after all. He tried another tactic. "Boomer got a thorn under his paw. I had to take him to the vet to remove it."

Bingo. That got her attention. Concern wrinkled her brow as she looked up at him. "Is he all right?"

"It was a pretty big thorn." Under a microscope maybe. "He's been limping around, looking for sympathy and a little extra attention."

*Kind of like me,* Reese thought.

"I'm sure he'll be fine." She smiled at Melanie and Gabe, who danced by holding Kevin in their arms.

"I don't know," Reese mused. "Sometimes when

something gets under the skin like that, it can turn into something serious."

"He's a tough little dog," she said evenly. "He'll bounce back in no time."

"He misses you." Reese pulled her closer, felt her stiffen. "I miss you."

"Reese—"

"Tell me what to say, Syd." When she put her hand on his chest, he felt panic grip his throat. "Please, just tell me what to say."

She looked up at him then, and for a split second his pulse jumped; he was certain he saw something in her eyes: a need, longing. But then it was gone. Once again her eyes were cool and blank, and he knew it had just been wishful thinking.

"We've said everything already, Reese," she said quietly, then stepped out of his hold. "Excuse me, I need to say goodbye to Melanie and Gabe before I leave."

The song turned to a fast beat again, a Donna Summer disco song. Sydney disappeared into the throng of jumping bodies on the dance floor. He started to follow her, then stopped. Like the beat of the music, her words pounded in his brain.

*I'd like us to be friends, if that's all right.*

*A few flowers and I'm sorry's won't make it okay.*

*We've said everything already.*

Eyes narrowed, hands balled into fists, he turned and made his way back to his beer.

Six inches fell during the night, a white blanket of fluffy snow that sparkled in the early-morning light. From her bedroom window, Sydney watched the sun peek over the tops of John Gelson's maple trees. The branches were bare now, the brilliant colors of fall already yielded to the white of winter.

Like those branches, she felt stripped bare, cold. Empty.

Good Heavens. She turned away from the window and laughed at herself, shook her head at the absurdity of her thoughts. She'd promised herself she wasn't going to think about Reese today. She'd thought about him all night; dreamed of him even when she'd finally managed to fall asleep sometime in the wee hours of the morning.

She'd known better than to go to the reception last night, but Melanie and Cara and Abby had all been so insistent that she hadn't been able to refuse them. She'd thought that she could avoid Reese, mix with the other guests and keep her distance from him. He'd caught her off guard by dragging her out onto the dance floor like he had.

When he'd pulled her into his arms, it had taken every ounce of willpower not to give in to him. When he'd told her he missed her, she'd nearly thrown her arms around him and kissed him right there, in front of everyone.

But he hadn't said the words she needed, and she knew he never would. The mistake had been hers, trusting him, falling in love, foolishly believing, if only for a moment, that he might love her back.

Marry her.

Well, enough of feeling sorry for herself. She reached for her robe. A streusel muffin would take her mind off Reese, she decided. She'd bake up, oh, say, ten or twelve dozen, then maybe whip up a couple of hundred chocolate chip cookies, then a few dozen oatmeal raisin or—

She jumped at the sound of the ringing phone. No one called at seven-thirty on a Sunday morning. Her heart beat furiously as she stared at the phone.

Reese might.

She reached for the phone, then pulled her hand back. She wouldn't talk to him. She waited, breath held, when her machine clicked on, listened while her announcement played....

"Sydney, this is Cara...please, if you're there, pick up...there's been an accident...."

# Twelve

"Sydney, I'm so glad you're here."

Cara hurried down the hospital corridor toward her, and the women hugged briefly.

"How is he?" Sydney asked, glancing worriedly at the hospital door Cara had just stepped out of.

"Lots of scrapes and bruises, and a mild concussion. The doctors said he can go home in a couple of hours and he should be fine in a few days. Lord, he scared the bejesus out of all of us. Come on—" she took Sydney's arm and dragged her toward the room "—one smile from you ought to cheer him up. He's been very cranky with everyone since they brought him in an hour ago."

"Do you really think I should go in?" Sydney didn't want to intrude on a family gathering. "He might not feel like having company, especially so soon, and I could—"

But Cara was already pulling her through the door. Callan and Ian stood beside the bed, laughing as if someone had just told a joke, and Abby was shaking her head at them while she filled a glass with ice water.

Lying in bed, dressed in a blue hospital gown, one large bandage on his temple, was Lucian.

Everyone went quiet when she entered the room; Sydney shifted nervously, then looked at Lucian, felt her stomach twist as she took in the scrapes and bruises covering his arms and left side of his face. "How are you feeling?"

A smile touched his mouth, but the pain in his blurry eyes was evident. "I'm sure a kiss would make it all better," he suggested.

Abby rolled her eyes and handed the glass of water to Lucian, then moved toward Sydney and gave her a hug. "That's what he said to the nurse fifteen minutes ago, just before she stuck him in the butt with a needle."

Sydney moved beside the bed and placed a gentle kiss beside the bandage on Lucian's forehead. He closed his eyes and sighed. "Now I can die a happy man."

"He said that to another nurse when she fluffed his pillow a few minutes ago," Cara said dryly.

The Sinclair men, Sydney thought with a smile. There wasn't a woman who was safe around them. She knew firsthand. Her smile faded as she glanced around the room. "Reese isn't here yet?"

"I finally got hold of him about ten minutes ago," Cara said. "He'll be here any minute."

When Cara hadn't been able to reach Reese at the cottage or the tavern to tell him about Lucian's accident, she'd called Sydney, thinking maybe he'd spent the night at her place. Sydney didn't want to know where

Cara had finally found Reese. Didn't want to know if he'd spent the night with someone. She was still too fragile to think about him being with another woman, holding her, kissing her. Making love to her.

Pain squeezed her chest at the thought. She wouldn't think about Reese now. She was here for Lucian. Lightly she covered his hand with her own. "What happened?"

Lucian shook his head, then winced at the movement. "Damned if I know. The last thing I remember is toasting Gabe and Melanie at the reception. Next thing I know I'm lying in this bed with the Headache from Hell."

"They found him at Jordan's Junction, unconscious in his truck," Ian said. "It appears that he skidded on some ice and went over the side of the road."

"What in the world he was doing at Jordan's Junction at six-thirty in the morning remains a mystery." Cara folded her arms, trying to look stern and reprimanding, but the worry in her eyes was plain, as was the relief that her brother was going to be all right.

"Do Gabe and Melanie know?" Sydney asked.

Cara shook her head. "They left after the reception for a red-eye flight out of Philly. Right about now I figure they're having breakfast on a beach in St. Thomas."

"Sure they are." Callan looked at the other men, who all grinned knowingly.

Cara rolled her eyes. "So okay, they're having breakfast in their room. In any event, we all decided, since Lucian is all right, not to tell them until they get back in two weeks."

"Gabe's not gonna like it."

All heads turned at the sound of Reese's voice from the doorway.

At the sight of him standing there, Sydney's throat went dry as dust. He still wore his tuxedo, minus the cummerbund and bow tie. His hair hadn't been combed; he hadn't shaved and his eyes looked glassy.

He looked as if he'd been out all night.

Sydney swallowed, followed his gaze down to where her hand was still touching Lucian's. She noticed a twitch at the corner of one weary eye, but when he moved into the room, he had his attention on Lucian, not her. She slipped her hand from Lucian's and moved away from the bed.

Reese nodded at his brother. "You all right?"

"Pretty nurses to fluff my pillow and beautiful women at my bedside." Lucian lifted one brow, then winced at the movement. "Maybe I did die and go to Heaven."

Reese frowned. "Not funny, Bro. I saw your truck as it was being towed away. It looks about as pretty as your face right now."

"Damn," Lucian growled. "I liked that truck, too."

As the banter continued, Sydney inched her way toward the door and slipped out. She was halfway down the hallway, struggling not to break into a run. Emotions were running too high right now. For her, for Reese. He'd been out all night, she knew. It was obvious. It could just as easily have been him lying on the side of an icy road somewhere. Only maybe he wouldn't have been as lucky as Lucian. When he'd walked into the hospital room, she'd wanted to throw herself in his arms and kiss him, tell him that she loved him.

Thank God she hadn't.

"Sydney. Wait."

She stopped at the sound of Cara's voice, closed her eyes on a sigh, then opened them again as she turned.

"Come have a cup of herbal tea with me. After all this excitement, my child and I need a little something to calm us down." Cara smiled and pressed a hand to the slight bulge on her stomach. When Sydney hesitated, Cara took her arm. "Please."

They walked to the hospital cafeteria and sat down with two steaming cups of hot water and tea bags. Cara stared at hers while it steeped, then said, "You know he loves you, don't you?"

Sydney glanced up sharply. "What?"

Cara raised her cup, blew on the hot liquid. "Men can be such...well, men. They want to believe that they're the dominant creature and no one can ever control them, so they beat their chests and jump around like a bunch of monkeys. But when they're all done acting ridiculous, they come around and roll over like puppies."

Somehow Sydney didn't quite see Reese as a monkey or a puppy. When she'd been furious with him, though, she *had* thought of him as a donkey's behind. "You're wrong, Cara. He doesn't love me. What we had was—" she hesitated, felt the tears at the back of her throat "—was about sex," she whispered. "That's all."

"Don't kid yourself, Syd. I've never seen him look at a woman the way he looks at you. And believe me—" she smiled "—I've seen him look at a lot of women."

Sydney raised a brow. "I suppose that's intended to make me feel better?"

Cara laughed. "It's no secret that Reese has dated a lot of women. But it was always casual, never serious. And never, ever was he jealous. According to Lucian,

Reese nearly took his head off when he saw you two alone in your restaurant. And these past two weeks, Lord help us, sweet, never-let-anything-or-anybody-get-to-him Reese Sinclair has been a bear. A big, grumpy bear. And that, my dear, is *not* just about sex."

"There is something else," Cara said and leaned closer. "But he'd kill me if he knew I told you this. The night of the café's opening, the burners weren't down at the tavern. He sent everybody over from his place to yours, told them that their meals were on the house next time they came in, then he closed down. Believe me, there isn't another woman alive Reese would do that for."

"He did *what?*" Wide-eyed, Sydney stared at Cara.

"He doesn't think anyone knows," Cara said, sipping her tea. "But I suspected, so I ran a stealth operation and checked out his story. Every single burner was in perfect working order."

He'd done that? Lied about his burners being out and offered incentives to anyone who came over to her place? There *had* been an odd assortment of customers that night, she remembered, but she'd been too excited to consider that they hadn't come in on their own.

She pressed a shaky hand to her temple. She didn't know what to think, what to believe. It was possible that the burners had simply started working again. Maybe Corky or someone had fixed them. Cara could be wrong about everything.

Sydney couldn't believe any of it: the burners being out, that Reese was in love with her. She wanted to, but she couldn't. Couldn't risk the pain of letting herself believe that Reese loved her, only to learn the truth.

"Cara." Sydney sighed, shook her head. "Thank you. I know you're just trying to help, but it won't work between Reese and me. We had a…nice time together, but we're completely different people."

"You really believe that?" Cara asked.

"Absolutely." She would, Sydney told herself. She would believe it. "He'll go his way and I'll go mine. It's better that way for both of us."

"Okay, Syd." Cara shrugged, tucked a loose strand of blond hair back behind her ear. "Well, I'd better get back to check on Lucian. Thank the good Lord hard heads run in this family," she said as she stood. "It's the only thing that saved that boy."

Sydney stared at her tea long after Cara had left, long after the steam ceased to rise. She no longer felt like baking cookies or muffins, but she had pastries to make for tonight's desserts at the café, plus tables to set up, bread dough to prepare and an herb dressing for one of tonight's special salads.

She rose slowly, hugged her jacket tightly to her as she stepped out into the cold and headed back home.

"Tonight we have a pan-roasted white fish with garlic mashed potatoes and sautéed green beans, a grilled filet mignon with Yukon Gold potatoes…"

Sydney recited the evening's specials to Max and Eileen Brenner, who had already been to the café three times since the opening. In only two weeks, Sydney already had several repeat customers for dinner, plus several regulars at her lunch dining: ladies out for a social afternoon and businessmen and women who wanted to impress their clients with something a little nicer than a sandwich or hamburger from a coffee shop or Squire's Tavern.

Even her grandfather had conceded to her that she'd done a good job, though Sydney had nearly fallen over at his praise. Tonight he was at the café with a group of lawyers and their wives from Ridgeway, and she could hear him bragging about his granddaughter's cooking while Nell opened a bottle of wine for the table.

And all she wanted to do was sit down on the floor and cry.

She was thankful that the café was unusually busy this evening. Work was the only thing that kept her mind off Reese and what Cara had told her this morning at the hospital.

*He loves you.*

He didn't. She'd had all day to think about it, reason it out in a logical manner. In spite of what Cara said, Sydney was certain that the physical aspect of their relationship had been what attracted him to her, that's all. And she wanted more than that. A happy-go-lucky bachelor like Reese Sinclair didn't settle down and have kids with the uptight, snooty granddaughter of the Honorable Judge Randolph Howland. She would like to think that she'd relaxed a little, and that she didn't take life quite as seriously as she had, but she was basically the same person she'd always been. Whoever she *did* marry would have to love her exactly the way she was, with all her flaws and faults.

"I made an artichoke ravioli today with you both especially in mind," Sydney told Max and Eileen when she noticed Cara and Abby come into the café. "I'll have some sent over, on the house, while you decide what you'd like for dinner."

Sydney excused herself and made her way toward Cara and Abby, who waved at her, then seated themselves at a table that Sydney called her "last chance" table. It not only had a direct view of the main kitchen door, it was in the path of the servers coming in and out of the kitchen. She offered to move the women, but they just smiled and insisted they were fine.

"How's Lucian?" Sydney asked.

"They sent him home at noon," Cara said with a smile. "Probably to stop him from coming on to the nurses. Based on one cute little brunette he'd been flirting with, I have the feeling that he'll be receiving some at-home nursing care."

"Ian and Callan will be along shortly." Abby smoothed her napkin on her lap. "Before they get here, we were hoping we could talk to you about something."

"Well—" She glanced around the restaurant. Becky was at the front, and Nell and her new waitress, Susan, seemed to have everything under control. For the past twenty minutes, Sydney had been busy talking to customers and serving drinks, but Nell had reassured her— several times, in fact—that everything was fine in the kitchen and she wasn't needed there.

"I have a couple of minutes." She sat at their table, suddenly nervous what they might want to talk to her about. "But I've got to help serve as the orders come up."

"This won't take long," Cara said. "We need to talk to you about Reese."

Sydney felt her insides twist. "Cara, Abby, this really isn't—"

"It's serious," Abby whispered. "He's gone crazy."

"Crazy?" Sydney blinked. "What do you mean?"

"Right over the edge." Cara made a diving gesture with her hand. "We think he needs to be committed before he hurts himself."

"That's ridiculous." Sydney laughed, then frowned when both women stared at her, their expressions sober.

This was absurd. Ludicrous. She shook her head, then

went still when Reese opened the front door of the café and stepped in. He was wearing a tux, not the one from last night, but a clean, fresh one.

"Sorry I'm late, Syd," he said, moving toward her.

"Late?" She had no idea what he was talking about, or why he was wearing a tuxedo.

He turned away from her then and looked at Cara and Abby. "Good evening, ladies. Is there anything I can get for you this evening? A glass of wine, sparkling cider?"

*What in the world?...* Dumbstruck, all Sydney could do was stare.

"I'll have the cider, Abby will have the wine," Cara said smoothly.

He pulled an order form and pen out of his pocket and wrote it down. "Anything else? I made a lovely quiche tonight, with goat cheese and just a kiss of basil."

"Just the drinks for now." Cara casually picked up her menu and stared at it.

"Very good, then," he said in a most proper, stuffy waiter manner.

He turned away, headed for another table, when Sydney jumped up and tugged on his arm. "What do you think you're doing?" she growled between her teeth, though she had a smile frozen on her lips. He *had* gone crazy, she thought. Cara and Abby were right.

"Wasn't that the bet?" He looked at her with a puzzled expression in his green eyes. "I'm supposed to wear a tux, wait on tables and make quiche if I lost?"

The bet. He was owning up to losing. And *now,* of all times. "Reese, this isn't funny."

"We think it's hilarious," Cara muttered from behind

them, but Reese merely lifted a bored brow at her comment.

"I'm not trying to be funny," he said quietly, and gazed at her so intently she felt her chest tighten. "You should have won that game, Syd. I did cheat to teach you a lesson, and it got out of hand. I'm sorry. And now I'm holding up my end of the deal. What's right is right."

The determined look in his eyes told her that he wasn't going anywhere, and she hardly wanted to make a scene now. When he turned away from her again and moved to another table to take their order, she could only stare in disbelief.

Callan and Ian came in through the front door then and glanced at Reese. She noticed one corner of Ian's mouth twitch, but the men turned their attention to their wives, then joined them at their table.

This had to be one of those weird, doesn't-make-any-sense dreams, she decided. Nothing else could possibly explain the bizarre behavior going on around her. Certainly she'd wake up any minute, her heart racing, her palms sweating, gasping for breath.

Except she *was* awake, and her heart *was* racing, her palms sweating, her breathing labored.

She realized that everyone was looking at her, as if waiting for something to happen.

Well, she had a restaurant to run, she thought as she glanced at the kitchen and realized that it had been a long while since the door had opened and any orders had been brought out. Quite a long while, as a matter of fact. The last thing she needed was a problem in the kitchen. At the moment, she had more than she could handle out here.

She certainly didn't have time to stand around and

play this game with Reese, she fumed as she started toward the kitchen. If he wanted to wait on tables, fine. Let him wait on tables. But it wasn't going to change anything between them, not one thing at—

She stopped, then frowned when she pushed on the kitchen door and it didn't give. Wondering what else could go wrong tonight, she yanked the door open instead.

Roses.

Dozens and hundreds and *thousands* of roses of every color poured out from the kitchen. Startled, she stepped back, but lost her footing and went down on her bottom onto a soft blanket of petals and thornless stems.

When the river of roses stopped, she stared up at Reese, who stood over her, looking down.

Her eyes narrowed slowly. "You—you—" She grabbed a handful of roses and threw them at him. "You *are* crazy!"

"Certifiable." He knelt beside her, an amused grin on his face.

"Cara is right," she sputtered and threw another handful of flowers. "You should be committed."

"Okay." His grin faded. "I will if you will."

"Will what?" She blew a strand of hair out of her eyes, knew that everyone was looking at her.

"Be committed," he repeated. "To you, Syd. Only to you."

She stilled as he reached into his pocket and pulled out a black velvet box. His hand was as steady as his gaze as he handed it to her.

Her heart, which had stopped only a second before, now pounded furiously as she took the box. Her hands shook as she opened it.

A beautiful diamond solitaire sparkled on a shiny

gold band. The swelling in her chest made it impossible to speak.

"Will you marry me?" he asked in front of everyone there, including her staff, who'd all stopped in their work to come over and watch the show. Even Latona stood by, her chef's hat on, a spatula in her hand and her big brown eyes all dewy.

When Sydney didn't answer him, Reese felt his throat turn to dust. The thought that he might have lost her forever ripped at his insides. He was on shaky, unfamiliar ground here, and he could only let instinct and his heart guide him.

"I love everything about you, Syd," he said quietly. "The way your eyes light up when you smile, the sound of your laugh, your enthusiasm for life and for—" he paused, glanced around the room and thought he really shouldn't mention their lovemaking in front of all these people, especially her grandfather, who was staring very hard at him at the moment.

He swallowed hard and turned back to Sydney. "I even love that snobby little way you lift your nose at me when you think you know more than me."

"I do know more than you," she said, but there was no challenge in her words. She was still staring at the ring, her lips softly parted.

"Then you know I love you, that I need you more than my next breath," he said and took her hand in his, slipped the ring out of the box onto her finger. "Please marry me, Syd. Please."

The scent of roses filled the silent café. Reese held his breath; it seemed as if the entire room held its breath. She glanced up at him, stared with wide, tear-filled eyes.

"Yes," she whispered. "Yes, yes."

Her arms came around him as a cheer went up with the room. Whistling and clapping, silverware clinking against glasses. He scooped her up off the floor into his arms, kissed her deeply.

"Tell me you love me, too," he said against her lips. "I need to hear it."

Her arms tightened around his neck. "Of course I love you, you idiot."

He grinned at her. "Ah, the words every man longs to hear, other than, 'dinner's ready.'"

Smiling, she brought her lips to his. "I love you," she whispered. "It frightens me, I admit it, but I do love you. With all my heart."

Her words were like bubbles of champagne bursting in his chest. He'd never felt anything like this before, this *elated*. He wanted to laugh, go outside and dance in the snow, make love to her all night.

He kissed her again, thinking that a lifetime with this woman wouldn't be enough. He'd fought against his feelings for her from the first night she'd walked into the tavern, covered with mud, holding Boomer in her arms. He now realized he hadn't lost the battle, he'd won.

"We've got it covered here," Nell said, and the rest of Sydney's staff all nodded. "Why don't you two go celebrate?"

Applause went up from the room again. Reese looked at Sydney, who smiled, then nodded. Amidst more cheers and applause, Reese carried her outside, then up the back stairway that led to her apartment.

When he had her inside, alone, he set her down and drew her into a kiss. Long and slow, he tasted the sweetness of her, knew that she was what he wanted. What he would always want.

"You know that by tomorrow, the whole town will

be talking about you and me,'' he murmured between kisses.

"Let them talk.'' She eased back, looked up into his eyes. The love he saw in her steady gaze took his breath away. "As long as you love me, nothing can ever hurt me again.''

When she touched his cheek, he turned his head and kissed the palm of her hand, smiled when he felt her shiver.

"So tell me how you got all those roses in there without me knowing?'' she whispered, her voice breathless.

"It's a secret.'' He pulled her closer, loved the feel of her heart against his. "Maybe in fifty or sixty years, I'll tell you.''

Smiling, she stepped out of his arms and backed toward the bedroom. "I'll bet I could get you to tell me now.''

"Sweetheart,'' he said with a grin and followed, knowing that life with Sydney would never be dull, "that's definitely a bet I'd lose.''

\* \* \* \* \*

*There will be more*
SECRETS! *books coming soon.*
*But first, watch for*
*Barbara McCauley's contribution to*

*THE FORTUNES OF TEXAS:*
*THE LOST HEIRS,*

*coming in September*
*from Silhouette Desire.*

**SILHOUETTE® MAKES YOU A STAR!**

Look in the back pages of
all June Silhouette series books to find an
exciting new contest with fabulous prizes!
Available exclusively through Silhouette.

Don't miss it!

*Silhouette®*

Where love comes alive™

*P.S. Watch for details on how you can meet
your favorite Silhouette author.*

## Desire

January 2001
**TALL, DARK & WESTERN**
**#1339 by Anne Marie Winston**

February 2001
**THE WAY TO A RANCHER'S HEART**
**#1345 by Peggy Moreland**

March 2001
**MILLIONAIRE HUSBAND**
**#1352 by Leanne Banks**
Million-Dollar Men

April 2001
**GABRIEL'S GIFT**
**#1357 by Cait London**
Freedom Valley

May 2001
**THE TEMPTATION OF RORY MONAHAN**
**#1363 by Elizabeth Bevarly**

June 2001
**A LADY FOR LINCOLN CADE**
**#1369 by BJ James**
Men of Belle Terre

## MAN OF THE MONTH

For twenty years Silhouette has been giving you the ultimate in romantic reads. Come join the celebration as some of your favorite authors help celebrate our anniversary with the most sensual, emotional love stories ever!

*Available at your favorite retail outlet.*

*Silhouette®*
*Where love comes alive™*